FATAL

Stupid in love

Nileyah Mary Rose

Izzy V Productions

ISBN-13:9798737070519
ISBN-10: 1477123456

Cover design by: Art Painter
Library of Congress Control Number: 2018675309
Printed in the United States of America

CHAPTER 1

The music echoed through the house while bodies swayed with the rhythm vibrating from their feet. It was a night before graduation and Tony's house was the place to be. Tony was what you would call a "fuck boy." He was handsome, and he knew it. Girls effortlessly swallowed his bullshit because of his sexy appearances. In high school, a party at Tony's is where you would want to be. He knew everyone and everyone knew him. Tony planned his graduation party to be one that is unforgettable; he even themed it 'The End of an Era'.

It was 9pm when Sia walked into the party. She was a senior and she couldn't miss the last Tony Shaffer party that their high school will ever see. She would have dragged her best friend Davina with her even if she was on her deathbed. Davina's boyfriend Allen and his best friend Clay tagged along with the girls. Clay may prove to be an obstacle for Sia's motives tonight. Limitless shots and drinking games continued to flow throughout the night; thanks to Tony's plan to get everyone at his party as inebriated as possible. After all, a good tale of a formidable function is equal to how much you don't remember. His mission seemed accomplished as bodies of teenagers and young adults scattered through every surface of his mansion. Everyone seemed to find a place where they could indulge in their sins. The air was thick and warm filled with cheap cigarette smoke. It was a true scene of drunken teenagers and carbon monoxide filled air clinging to sticky sweaty skin. Some engaged in drinking games while others gathered in secluded corners smoking marijuana. Some were getting to know each other while others danced the night away. Everyone was having the time of their lives.

Sia looked across the room to see Tony surrounded by a group of thirsty girls as usual and they weren't thirsty for another drink of tequila with lime. Tonight, will be her night; it had to be since they were graduating high school the next day, with everyone going their separate ways. Sia didn't know if she would ever get this chance again. Her only reason for coming was to finally speak to him. She remembered when she first met Tony; it was during sophomore year in her math class with Mr. Kits. Tony had recently transferred to the school. Sia was looking down at her book as she always did, trying to avoid the blazing stare of Pete's Raters. She could feel him staring so hard that she could feel it like the wind blowing in a storm. Rumors were that Pete liked her and planned on asking her out any day now. She always made herself look busy so that he wouldn't want to approach her. It wasn't that Pete was not sexy or attractive; in fact, he was rather handsome. He played basketball and girls liked him. But Sia played hard to get which made him want her even more. "Class we have a new student." Mr. Kits cleared his throat as he continued to introduce Tony to the class. This was the first time Sia looked up all period. " His Name is Tony Bellamy and his family just moved out here from California."

Back to scene - Graduation Party

Clay approached Sia who was standing alone looking across the room, staring at Tony's every move.

"Wanna dance?"

"No Thanks," Sia said nonchalantly as she walked away towards the open bar to fill up her red cup. "Sia?" Nita approached her.

"Oh, hey girl…" Sia said as she swallowed the drink in her mouth.

"I thought you said you weren't coming," Nita said.

"Well here I am." she said with an innocent chuckle and a half-smile.

"Have you talked to him?"

"Who?" Sia said while pouring the drink into her mouth, trying to avoid the conversation they were about to have.

"You know who…don't play dumb."

"Tony?"

"Who else?" she said as she smiled through a mild frown. Nita always had this way of sarcastically responding instead of being straight with her answers.

"No, he is pretty occupied right about now." she said with her eyebrow raised then she raised her liquor to her mouth.

"You are almost out of high school, so stop acting like…" Sia cut her off.

"Like what?" she responded.

"Like a shy and innocent little kid."

"I'm not" Sia almost lost her voice.

"Then why are they in his face and not you? Girl the only way to get what you want is to claim what's yours."

"I'm good, just having fun."

"Ok, fine if that's how you want it." Nita said as she turned around and walked away. Sia thought to herself for a second then waited until Tony stepped away to get a drink. She courageously poured the rest of her liquor in her mouth before approaching him while he was at the drink counter reaching for a cup.

"Nice party." she said nervously.

"Thank you!" Tony said as he stared her down while licking his lips. She blushed. "What's your name?" he asked. She could feel his eyes undressing her.

"Sia."

"And I'm…" he was reaching for a handshake

"I know who you are." she cut him off before he could finish.

"Oh do you now?"

"Pretty much."

"That hardly seems fair. Since you know who I am, why haven't you said hello or something?"

"I'm saying something now, hi…" she said with a smile, trying not to show that she was nervous. Her hands were sweating, and her stomach started tingling like she was riding a roller coaster at its dropping point.

"Right…right…" he said then continued "well it's nice to finally to meet you face to face Sia." Tony reached out his hand.

"It's nice to meet you too." She met his hand.

"Well since you already know me, I would like to get to know you." His eyes got more intensified on her as she became nervous all over again.

"We can arrange that." she said with a smile.

"What a terrible host!" That was the sound of a sloppy drunk girl approaching him as she wrapped her arms around his waist from behind. Tony turned his head and looked at the girl and responded, "I'm sorry, I'm just talking to a guest." He said as he then turned to look at Sia with a smile. Sia saw all the progress she just made with him in those five minutes vanished right before her eyes. "Well, there are more guests out there to mingle and chat with so come on!" she said while pulling him away.

"Sorry, I will be right back." Tony whispered lifting a finger while being pulled away,

Sia was disappointed. She finally took a chance at making a move with Tony only to have some 'Hoe' get in her way. She thought as she looked around for Nita. She knew Nita was watching the entire time waiting for her chance to hear all of the details. She cited Nita and walked to her swaying from the blurriness of her eyesight. She was starting to feel the liquor meet her blood stream. "See... I tried."

"You actually spoke to him?" Nita asked as if she never saw anything.

"Yes, I did."

"And... What happened?"

"Some drunk idiot interrupted us." Sia said as she purposely left out the fact that Tony smiled at her too. This was her way of getting Nita to feel sorry for her.

"Well the night is still young; you can still get more of his time if you want. But for now, let's drink up." she lifted her cup that was still half full.

"Now, that I can do." They drank and danced with no more care in the world. Sia's mission was ruined, so she turned to alcohol to make it all better. Despite her failed mission, she still had reasons to celebrate. She was graduating with a 4.0 GPA and she finally spoke to Tony who she drooled over for nearly two years.

She spotted Davina who was making out with her boyfriend, barely hanging onto the side of the couch. She stumbled her way over to where they were at and squeezed herself in between them. Allen, Divina's boyfriend moved away with irritation as Davina laughed at the site of her best friend. She couldn't believe she had turned into the girl you babysit at a party.

"Oh my God Sia are you drunk?"

"Me? No never!!"

"Fucking Liar! You are sloppy drunk right now," she said with a laugh.

"Hey, babe you ready to go? "Allen said, hoping to finish what they had started after getting rid of everyone they came with.

"Yeah we can," she said as she looked at him and he could tell they were on the same page. Davina turned to Sia. "Let's go."

"Where?" Sia slurred out her words.

"Home you drunk bitch, where else?" she said with a smile as Allen got up and walked out with Clay.

"But it's not that late, I'm not ready to go!" she said as she wobbled and landed on Davina again. Sia wanted to stay so that she could talk to Tony again, but she knew she was in no shape to do that.

"You are too drunk to make any fucking decisions, get your ass up."

"I am not drunk, stop saying that."

"Ok sure." She said as she pulled her up to go.

"You guys are leaving?" Nita said as she saw Davina helping Sia out of the door

"Yeah, she still can't handle her liquor." she said as they both laughed.

"Now you see why we don't let her drink."

"Hey I can handle my liquor!" Sia interrupted.

"Sure you can." Davina mocked.

"Who is driving?" Nita asked.

"Not her!" They both laughed in unison.

"I can drive."
"Yeah right, definitely not on my watch."
"She thinks I'm drunk," Sia said to Nita.
"But you are." She said with a laugh.
"I can still drive! it's my car!!"
"And this is my life behind these wheels!!! Let's go..." Davina said as she pulled her out of Tony's house, towards the car.

CHAPTER 2

The rain was falling hard, and Allen was driving Sia's car. Everyone in the car fell asleep. Davina was in the back of the seat with Sia; Clay was in the front with Allen. Suddenly, Allen made a wrong turn down the one-way street; all he saw was bright lights, a loud crash with screeching tires as his face hit the steering wheel. Allen opened his eyes and realized he hit a car head-on; "Oh fuck!" escaped from Allen's lips. He was tipsy and his focus was blocked. He didn't even see the other car coming before making that turn. Everyone woke up in shock except for Sia; she was still passed out in the back seat but clearly breathing.

Allen came out of the car with blood on his forehead coming down his shirt. Everyone got out of the car except for Sia. Davina rushed to Allen and hugged him as he pulled away from her to approach the car he just hit.

He walked toward the car in front of them to see if the other passengers were okay. As Allen approached the vehicle, he saw a clearly pregnant woman.

"Miss.... excuse me miss are you okay?" Allen asked the woman realizing she was unresponsive. So much blood covered her face that he couldn't even tell you what color the woman's hair was.

"FUCK!!!" he yelled out of panic.

"Allen...what?" Davina heard his panic and ran to him.

"Oh my God, oh my God, oh my God!" She said as she burst out in tears.

"We've got to go right now." Allen said, pulling Davina to the side.

"G-g-g-g-go where? We can't go; we need to call the police. There is blood everywhere!!!" she said as tears rushed down her face mixing with the blood that rubbed on her cheek after hugging

Allen.

"And say what? Look I can't go to jail for this shit."

"This is Sia's car; the police will come after her."

"They wouldn't have to if she is still on the scene when they get here."

"What are you saying?" she said as she frowned through her tears.

"Look baby it's Sia. She is a sweet innocent girl; she will probably just get a slap on the wrist."

"Allen we can't just leave her here to take the blame."

"Your father is the best attorney in town, he will get her out. She will be fine; baby let's just go please." She kept quiet. Even with the thunder and lightning, everything was still silent to her. "There is so much blood, so much blood. Davina kept saying to herself repeatedly. She wanted it all to just be a dream with her lying in bed with Sia joking about how she can't hold liquor. Davina was going to walk downstairs and get a bowl of cereal while she waited for Sia to wake up. She loves Sia's house; She was always there, so Sia's mom eventually presented her with a house key in a tiny pink box with a white ribbon. Davina remembers Sia being so happy that day. She thought it had something to do with Tony; it was always a Tony thing these days with her. Sia was more excited watching Davina open the box. She heard Sia's mom say, "I told her not to make a big deal out of it." She drove to Allen's house that day and lay in bed next to him, talking about how Sia and her will be moving in together in whatever college they do agree to go to.

Allen came close to his girlfriend, he grabbed her face and pulled himself closer to her.

"Do you love me" Davina could only hear every other word.

"Yes," she almost shouted so she could hear her own voice.

"I can't go to jail baby."

"I don't want you to." She couldn't even look Allen in his eyes.

"But somebody will have to take the fall. Sia has the best shot at beating this. Baby look, I'm a black man they will not give it two thoughts to throw my black ass in jail. Please, baby please, I'm scared. I don't want to go to jail." He said as Sia was still in the car motionless.

"Come on y'all, we have to go before people see us here," Clayton said while getting up off the curb he was sitting on.

"Can't you see me talking to my girl?" Allen said furiously, and then turned to Davina "What do you want to do? If we stay, I'm going to jail. Is that what you want huh?"

"No, I don't." she said with tears in her eyes.

"Then choose and do it now because we don't have time." Davina thought for a second then replied, "I'm so sorry Sia," she said looking at Sia's direction with tears pouring down her cheek. "Now what?"

"Now you will have to stay behind."

"What?" Davina said, she was confused about what Allen had planned.

"That's the only way they will believe our story. We can't all just disappear; we need someone who can recall the event."

"So you want me to stay here with her?" she said with fright in her tone.

"Yes, Davina. Look, we don't have time for this, all you need to do is lie on the passenger's side and keep your eyes closed until the police come."

"Ok," she was numb. This wasn't happening, this isn't real they will all wake up and everything will be fine. Davina's thoughts weren't making her feel better.

"But what about them?" she said pointing towards the other car of the pregnant woman.

"I will call the police from a pay phone as soon as I get to one."

"No, she won't make it. Call from your phone."

"They will know I was here."

"Block your number, we can't leave her like this."

"Ok... ok, I will. Now go."

"No...you call first."

"Okay, not here. I can't give them any reason to put me on the scene. You must trust me."

"I do. Just help her, please."

"I promise I will, but baby we need to put her in the driver's seat first before we go."

Davina watched as Clay and Allen pulled Sia from the back seat and positioned her at the driver's seat.

Allen wrapped the seat belt around her which almost woke her up as Sia adjusted her body a little. They both froze as Allen saw his whole plan unfolding and clearly, he was panicking. Sia finally lay still. Allen let out a quiet sigh of relief and quickly but gently strapped in her seatbelt. Allen then wiped his blood off the steering wheel with a handkerchief he always carried around in his back pocket. They saw emergency lights coming in their direction from a distance.

"See, somebody already called for help. We got to go, see you soon." Allen whispered to Davina, then kissed her on the cheek as him and Clay unsuspiciously walked away.

"Ok."

"I love you."

"I love you too," she said as she watched him leave before sitting in the car with Sia. "I'm so sorry Sia, I didn't mean to do this to you. You will get through this." she sobbed holding her best friend's hand. "I will find a way to get you out of this, I promise." Davina truly meant it. This was her best friend, her sister. She heard the ambulance coming closer and closer. *When will this nightmare be over?* she thought to herself while shaking out of control. Davina took control of herself. "Please forgive me!" she said as the ambulance got closer. Sia heard the siren noise, but she was still unconscious. She also heard Davina say, 'please forgive me'.

The paramedic ran to both cars as they quickly rushed the pregnant woman into an ambulance bed and immediately rushed her to the hospital. They came to Sia's car as they tried waking both of them up. "What's going on?" Davina said frantically, playing her role.

"You ok ma'am?" the police officer at the scene said to Davina as she looked around in panic.

The other paramedic rushed to Sia and pulled her out of the car.

 "You Ladies were in a car accident. Do you remember what happened?" one of the police officers questioned.

"No how? What happened?" She said, still playing her role.

"We are not quite sure, but it looks like your friend turned on a one-way street."

"Oh my God no! are they ok?" she said while pointing at the other vehicle like this was her first time seeing the car.

"We are hoping so. But we will need to take you in too, to make sure you're ok. "

"I'm fine. But is my friend ok?"

"She should be. They are taking her in now."

"I'm coming with her." Sia was rushed to the hospital.

CHAPTER 3

They got there and started IV on her immediately to get her hydrated. Davina stayed until the police officer came in. "Hello Miss Martin, my name is Officer Carter. How are you feeling?"
"I'm fine."
"That's good to know. Do you mind coming to the station with me for questioning?"
"For what?" She said out of fear.
"I will let you know when we get there. It will be brief."
"Ok..." she said, afraid of the fact that she was going to the police station. She wanted to talk to Allen first to tell her what to say, but she didn't want to draw any attention to him since she was with Officer Carter.
 She got to the station as they escorted her to the interrogation room "Do you want anything to drink?"

"No." she said, trying to prevent herself from shaking.

"Are you ok?" Officer Carter asked seeing how frightened she was.

"Yes, I'm just not used to being in here."

"Ok, well let's get started and get you on your way."

"Ok."

"So, tell me what happened about the accident."

"I don't know, I was asleep."

"Where were you both coming from?"

"From um, a party." she said as the officer was writing down her statement.

"Around what time did you both leave?"

"Like around 2AM."

"Who else was in the car with you two?"

"Huh? I mean it was just two of us." She said, trying to stick with the story they made up.

"Just you two?"

"Yes" she said as he continued to write.

"Did you know Miss Sia Moore was under the influence?"

"Yes."

"Why did you let her drive when you know she was under the influence?"

"I told her not to drive, that we can wait until we both sober up. But she didn't listen."

"So, you were under the influence too?"

"Yes."

"Ok well thank you for your time, that's really all for now; I will be in touch."

"Ok. Any news about the woman from the other vehicle?"

"Unfortunately, she passed away on her way to the hospital."

"Nooooo... nooooo" Davina burst out in tears with her hands covering her face "I am so sorry..."

"It's not your fault, we will keep in touch; you're free to go."

"Oh my God!! Noooo... and the child she was carrying too?"

"He survived. They got him out right on time."

"Oh, thank God" she said, still crying as the officer gave her a tissue and didn't interrupt her while she cried her eyes out.

"I can take you home anytime you are ready." They left the station and he drove her straight home. Davina pretended to ring the doorbell and waited on the front porch until the officer pulled away. She then jumped into her car that was in the driveway and left. Her mother was upstairs still in bed and her father wasn't living there anymore; her parents got a divorce when she was a sophomore.

CHAPTER 4

She drove straight to Allen's house who was in nothing but his sweatpants. He was sitting on the couch watching tv with no care in the world about what just happened.

Davina banged on the door which made Allen paranoid. He checked through the window to see who it was before attempting to open the door. "She died!!" She yelled out the moment he opened the door.

"Keep your fucking voice down while you're outside." He charged at her with a frown in his face.

"I'm sorry" she said while on edge.

"So, who died, the lady?" He asked.

"Yes, the lady." She said with her eyes boiling up in tears again.

"That's too bad; I wish I could tell the family sorry for their loss, but I can't." He shrugged his shoulders and went back to watching TV.

"Are you serious right now?"

"What do you want me to say? What's done is done!!"

"You are such an asshole." she said as she turned towards the door, ready to exit with different types of emotions running through her at once.

"Ok wait... Wait!!" He said louder realizing Davina wasn't going to stop upon his first request. "I'm sorry she died; I didn't mean for that accident to happen." He said, then continued "The baby passed away too?"

"No thank God" she said as she wiped her tears.

"Well look at the bright side, the child made it."

"Yes, the child that will grow up without his mother. Who's to say she didn't have other kids or a husband? She had a family that she was forced to leave behind because of us!"

"You are worrying too much about the things you cannot control Davina. She is gone! All we can do is pray for her living family and her baby that we do know about."

"Since when do you pray?"

"I pray, you just don't know when I do it." he replied proudly.

"So now what?"

"Now we live our lives like nothing ever happened." he said while facing her with a smile on his face.

"So, you want us to just go on with our lives and forget about my best friend and the trouble she is about to be in?"

"Yes. That's the plan. Now are we going to have an issue with you keeping that secret?" he said coming closer to her as she backed away feeling a little threatened.

"N... no... "she stuttered, afraid of what he may do to her.

"Good" he said as he leaned over and kissed her. She pulled back and walked away to his room. She was angry at everything and everyone, including herself for letting it happen the way it did.

 "Shouldn't you be getting ready for your graduation?" he walked in, then took off his sweatpants to get in the shower.

"No, it doesn't feel right going after what just happened."

"Why not, it's still your graduation day."

"I'm not going! So, leave it alone."

"Ok baby calm down, I'm sorry."

"So am I" she said as she got up and started putting the clothes, she left there inside a duffle bag that were in the closet by her things.

"You going somewhere?" Allen said standing behind her wrapped in a towel.

"Is that a problem?"

"No not at all baby, I'm just a little concerned about you right now. You're all over the place with your emotions."

"How am I supposed to act right now Allen?"

"Normal if that's possible."

"I will be fine; I just need a break."

"From me?"

"From everyone!!" she said while walking out with frustration, letting the screen door slam behind her.

"Will she be a problem?" Clayton asked. He was standing behind the door eavesdropping in their conversation.

"She could be. But I'll take care of her if she gets out of hand." He said tightly, closing his fist.

"I can take care of her for you." Clayton said rubbing his hands together

"Don't touch her." He responded before walking back to his room to take a shower.

CHAPTER 5

Davina arrived home and quickly walked towards her room ignoring her mother who was in the living room? "What's going on? I've been calling you for hours."

"Well, I'm here now." She walked to her room.

"Davina!" her mother called following behind her

"Please leave me alone." she said as she slammed the bedroom door.

"No please talk to me. What happened? I haven't seen you since you left yesterday for that party; did something happen to you there?" She felt concerned.

"Nothing happened; I will talk to you about it later."

"Ok! but your graduation is in three hours, you should start getting ready now. You know how you take forever to get dressed."

"I am not going."

"Ok that's it!! What Happened?"

"Mom I don't want to talk about it." She said as tears started to form in her eyes."

"Wrong answer, start talking..." She got in her face with her heart beating fast, demanding answers from her daughter.

"We got into a car accident and the lady we hit is dead... She is dead mom!!" She burst out in tears

"What???" Her mother said coming to her aid in shock as she held her close to herself, while she cried even more.

"What happened sweetie, how did it happen?" her mother asked, she was in tears along with her.

"I... I... don't know!!" she said crying uncontrollably "I... I... was asleep."

"Who was driving?"

"Huh?"

"Who was driving Davina?"

"Si... Sia." she said, still sticking to her story.

"Oh God no..." she said in disbelief but also relieved that it wasn't Davina who was driving.

"Where is she now?"

"Still at the hospital."

"Is she ok?"

"She was still unconscious when I left."

"When was that?"

"This morning before I went to the station for questioning."

"For questioning?" her mother said out of range. "Why would they want to question you when you weren't the one driving."

"They just wanted to know what happened."

"They still don't have the right to question you without a parent or lawyer. Didn't you tell them your dad was a lawyer?"

"Mom no… that wasn't important, I didn't do anything to involve a lawyer."

"But you still should have at least let me know."

"I know… I'm sorry. I just wasn't focused because I was worried about the mother, the baby and Sia."

"There was a baby involved too?" she said as her eyes got wider.

"Yes, she was pregnant."

"What???"

"Yes, but the baby is ok. They were able to get the baby out in time."

"Oh my God this is really serious."

"I know..." Davina's tears still wouldn't let up. At this point she was a complete mess. Her face was swollen like somebody gave her a black eye. Her makeup smeared all over her shirt and her hair was shaggy and knotted.

"Ok, ok, we will let your dad handle this. Come on, let's get you dressed for your graduation."

"I don't want to go; I don't feel right going after all that just happened.

"Davina, I know you're upset but I'm not going to let you miss your graduation after all the fights and struggle we went through just for you to pass." She sighed and lowered her tone as she continued. "Look... I understand what you are going through right now, but you cannot miss your graduation. We will figure it out after your graduation is done. We will get your dad on board to help Sia with whatever she needs."

"I don't need a lawyer too?"

"What for? You weren't driving. Unless you are not telling me everything that happened."

"I did. That's all."

"Are you sure?"

"Yes, momma that's all."

"Ok... Let's get ready for your graduation, we will figure the rest out later."

"Can I lie down for a little while? I am so tied." she said with exhaustion.

"Sure baby. But we need to start getting dressed within the next couple of hours."

"Ok" she said, trying to force herself to close her eyes, but couldn't. Everything that just transpired started to play in her head repeatedly. She couldn't fight it off, she just sat there and cried about it.

Over an hour has passed and she couldn't close her eyes. She was furious about Allen's reaction. "What a complete ass!" she said to herself. "How could he not care when he's the one that did this?" she said to herself. She hated the monster inside of him and she hated that she never knew it was there. She loved Allen so she stuck to the plan that they initially agreed to. "Sweetie..." Mrs. Martin called out. Davina acted like she didn't hear her mom calling her.

"Vina... Wake up sweetie; we have to get ready now."

"ok" she said in a soft tone, pretending to have just woken up.

She got up, cleaned up her face and put on her graduation gown with the hat to cover her hair that she barely brushed. She didn't feel like going. Davina felt bad for going while her best friend was at the hospital about to face whatever they think she did when she wakes up.

"I'm ready." she said softly. She was weak and just wanted to go to sleep.

Her mother looked at her "Sweetheart, we've got to do something about this now. You can't go to your graduation like this."

"I don't want to go..."

"We have to go honey."

"Then I'm going like this." Davina replied nonchalantly.

"Ok but let me fix your face up a bit and brush your hair a tad bit more." Davina silently waited as her mother rushed to go grab her makeup. Her mother started to put makeup on her face as Davina sat there in her deepest thoughts of what happened last night.

"Everything is going to be fine." Mrs. Martin broke the silence. Davina kept quiet as she stared at the picture on the wall.

CHAPTER 6

Before the ceremony, Davina's friends came to hug her and congratulate each other. She tried her best to act as if nothing had happened and tried to hide her pain with a fake smile.

"Hey! Where is Sia?" Nita asked.

"Huh?" Davina replied while being caught off guard.

"I'll be back…sorry" she said as she ran off to the restroom. Nita watched with confusion. Her mother saw her and followed.

"Are you ok sweetie?"

"Not really mom, I don't want to be here"

"Ok, I need you to get it together and at least walk across that stage without fumbling. You're almost there. It'll be over soon."

"But mom…"

"But nothing Vina. I understand that you're going through something big right now, but just get it together until it's over. This is by far the most important day of your life and I can't allow you to miss it because you're upset about something that you didn't do." She said, as she wiped the tears off her daughter's face.

Davina shook her head in an "okay" response.

"No more of this Vina. You are bringing attention to yourself. Wait until the ceremony is over."

They went back out as Davina took a seat in her designated area. She looked straight ahead trying to avoid everyone's stare. The students were happy as they all contributed to the loud whispering noises from so much chatter in the building.

The ceremony started as the speakers gave awards to honor students and teachers. After the awards, the students took turns walking across the stage and grabbing their diploma. When Davina's row was called, everyone got up except for her. She was in such deep thought that she didn't even hear her name called through the loudspeakers. She jumped as someone tapped her shoulder in efforts to get her attention.

"Oh, thank you." She got up and quickly joined her row mate. She got to Mrs. Anderson, one of the teachers who stood on stage. She grabbed her diploma from her and walked off without shaking the principal's hand who wanted to congratulate her like he did the others.

Everyone looked at how strange she'd been acting. She fixed a smile on her face while she was still very heavy at heart. She felt guilty for walking the stage at their graduation while her best friend was at the hospital waiting to be fingerprinted and booked for the crime she didn't commit.

When she got off the stage, she headed directly toward her mom's car and waited. She knew she had drawn attention to herself, but she didn't care; she wanted to leave.

"Hey sweetie!"

"Dad!!" Davina heard her dad's voice as she ran to his arms.

"It's going to be alright sweetheart" he said. Davina wouldn't release her tight hug. "Ok let's go, we will talk on the way home."

"Ok" she caught a ride with her Dad while her mom drove behind them. "Ok now tell me what's going on? I spoke with your mother and she told me what happened. I need to hear from you what really happened last night."

"Dad I didn't mean to..." she said as her eyes started to water a little bit.

"You didn't mean to what?"

"Umm, I didn't mean to let Sia drive while she'd been drinking at the party." She said changing her story.

"So that's what happened?"

"Yes!"

"How did it happen? Why didn't she see the lady's car coming?"

"I don't know, I was asleep. I told her not to drive and that we should rest up for a bit."

"So, she just ignored you and drove anyway and hit the lady?" He asked.

"Yes."

"Ok then, you did all that you could. You're not at fault. I'll help Sia as much as I can sweetie, but quite frankly…. there's not much that I can do for her Vina."

"Please do what you can dad, I don't want her to go to jail."

"Well, that's what happens when you act irresponsibly."

"It wasn't her fault"

"Then whose fault was it?" he asked in confusion. Now he was in attorney mode. He was so focused that he stopped pressing the gas and the car started to slow down. "Is there something you aren't telling me?"

"No… no… I told you everything."

"Ok. Just know you can't hide anything from me young lady. Everything comes to the light eventually, so I suggest you be honest with me now before things spiral out of control. Everything that I know about this accident is what will allow me to help you both."

"I know." Davina sighed and laid her head against the window.

CHAPTER 7

The Doctor approached David (Lisa-the victim's husband). Surrounded by both family members, he was pacing back and forth. "Mr. Freeman?" the nurse called out. Everyone brought their attention to her.

"Yes, it's me. How is she? Is she ok?" he asked anxiously with Lisa's mother behind him.

"I am so sorry Mr. Freeman, but we did everything we could." Doctor Ivie said.

"No don't you say that!" he said pointing his finger to her face "DON'T YOU FUCKING SAY THAT TO ME!" he burst out in tears and dramatically fell to the floor. "You can't say that to me" he said a third time crying.

"My daughter is dead?" Lisa's mother Rena joined in with her son in-law.

"I am so sorry." Doctor Ivie replied.

"Oh God!!" Rena said falling apart "What about my grandbaby?" she said in tears.

"He made it; he is in the Intensive Care Unit right now."

"Is he going to be ok?"

"Yes, he's going to be just fine. He's lucky to be alive."

"Can we see him?"

"Of course," the doctor led the way as David's mother picked him up.

"Come and see your son" Rena said. David was devastated and

didn't know what to do. They went to the ICU to see the baby boy attached to multiple wires. "Oh my God" David broke down again as the rest of the family, including Rena broke down seeing the baby in that condition.

"He will be ok. He is a true fighter" the Doctor said trying to comfort them.

David went home without the baby to relieve the nanny. He couldn't take him home yet; he was still in intensive care.

 Days went by without his baby boy. Amelia, their six-year-old daughter, and David were alone at home. He didn't take her to school, and he didn't go to work. He just sat there miserable and nonfunctional.

"I want my mommy!" Amelia said. She didn't understand what her father told her about her mother being dead.

"Just go to your room Amelia" David said in frustration.

"No!" Amelia said, refusing.

"Don't make me say it again."

"I want mommy!!"

"Your mother is dead, and she is never coming back!" he said in a louder tone this time.

"No... I hate you" she said as she burst into tears while running away towards her room.

"Amelia wait... I'm sorry. I didn't mean..." he said feeling sorry for hurting her with his words. Amelia ran to her room and covered her head with her pink Barbie duvet and started to cry. David came to sit next to her. He took a breath before speaking.

"I'm hurting too, baby. I wish I could bring her back to us, but I can't" he sighed.

"I don't care, just go!" she said furiously. David got up and slowly walked away, not knowing what he could do to take her pain away. He sat in front of her door and cried his eyes out. Hours later, he fell asleep at the front of her door. He woke while it was still dark outside, he could only get a few hours of sleep. He sneaked in her room to see that she fell asleep. He went to the living room to pour a drink of scotch and cried while taking a large sip. "Why Lisa? Why us?" he said, taking the glass off his mouth "Why God?" he said sobbing.

The next day, he went to Amelia's room since she didn't come out that morning "Amelia?" David said approaching her.

"Go away..."

"You can't be in here all-day baby girl."

"Leave me alone!!"

"What would you like to eat? I can bring you something." She fell silent refusing to eat.

"Ok, but you have to eat something eventually today."

"LEAVE ME ALONE!!!" she screamed as David closed her door behind him. He didn't know what to do. The next day he called the nanny to see if she could get her to eat. She didn't eat and remained in her room. Two days nearly went by before she finally came out of her room. "Daddy!" She was pale and fragile.

"Yes baby" he quickly got up to face her when he saw her.

"I want mommy." she passed out as her dad reached out and quickly caught her. "Amelia!!" David said, shaking her in panic. He quickly ran to the phone that was sitting on the breakfast bar while holding her and called 911.

"911 What's your emergency?"

"I need help.... please!"

"Okay, What's the emergency sir?"

"My daughter. Sh... She's not moving, and I don't think she's breathing...please hurry!"

"Ok calm down and tell me your address."

"1720 Walls Land Drive."

"Ok, the ambulances are on their way sir. I need you to stay calm and follow my lead."

"Ok!" he said panicking.

"Lay her flat on the floor."

"Ok" he did as instruct.

"Check on her pulse using her neck or wrist." He did and found no pulse.

"No pulse oh God!"

"You have to calm down and let me guide you through sir!"

"Ok, ok!" he said, wiping his tears.

"I need you to start CPR on her. I will guide you through it if you haven't done it before."

"I haven't done it before, but I think I can. I took the class for it once."

"Ok very good. Now start CPR on her until they get there. Put me on speaker and leave your door unlocked."

"Ok!" he ran to the door and unlocked it, then ran back and started doing CPR. He kept going until she finally responded with a breath of air."

"Dad!!" she said weakly with her eyes still closed.

"Shhhh it's ok, you will be ok." He heard the ambulance coming. He ran outside with her in her arms as the paramedics took over and rushed her to the hospital. He waited at the waiting room until the doctor came with news.

"Is she ok?" he said as he ran to the Doctor.

"Yes, she is. She was just dehydrated. Good job for taking her in on time."

"Oh, thank God!" he said with a sigh.

"We will keep her here up to 24 hours to make sure she gets enough fluids in her body."

"But she hasn't eaten for days."

"The fluids will help get her hydrated. We will make sure she eats when she wakes up."

"Ok thank you."

"Is everything okay at home for her to not want to eat?" The doctor asked in curiosity.

"We just lost her mother, and it has been hard on us all."

"Oh my God, I am so sorry for your loss."

"Thank you" he walked away to sit down. He ended up taking Amelia home the next day, while the baby was still in the hospital.

CHAPTER 8

Sia woke up in a room full of people; her hands were handcuffed to the hospital bed with her mother Carly who was sitting next to her. Carly quickly jumped up when she saw Sia moving. Her eyes slowly opened with a blur of confusion.

"Mom?" What's going on?" She said confused about why she was handcuffed to the hospital bed. She pulled her hands with the little strength she had left. She was feeling dizzy and unsure of what was going on.

"Sweetie, it's going to be ok. Your dad is on it, trust me. We already got a lawyer for you."

"A lawyer for what? What did I do? She spoke.

"Rest up baby it's going to be ok" she looked around to see her family member surrounding her with two officers by the door. She sat up with her heart beating fast.

"Please tell me what's going on."

"They think you were driving while under the influence and there was an accident behind it."

"What? An accident?"

"Yes. Rest up sweetie; we will talk about this when you're fully heal."

"No, I want to talk about it now. Why am I handcuffed to the bed?" Carly was silent with everyone else looking down afraid to tell her the truth. "Mom?"

"I can't!" Her mother said as she stomped out with one hand covering her mouth as she sobbed. Sia was so confused.

"What's going on? Somebody please tell me something!"

"The person that was involved in the accident died Sia." one of her aunts said. Her eyes got wider as she covered her mouth with the hand that was free of handcuffs. She wanted to be dreaming, but she knew she wasn't.

CHAPTER 9

David went back to the hospital, but this time to take his son home. His mother and nanny were at home helping with the kids, while David and Lisa's mom planned the funeral for his wife.

The day of the funeral was emotional; it was filled with pain and sorrow. Not one eye in that room was dry, including Amelia who was finally understanding that her mother wasn't coming back from the dead. Davina was also there, but she didn't want anyone to see her. She cautiously hid by the side of a nearby tree and watched them as they put her six feet under. She cried with the family even though she couldn't show her face.

CHAPTER 10

Sia was finally well enough to face the crime she thought she committed. She didn't remember, but according to Davina's story, she knew she did it. She believed in her heart that Davina wouldn't do anything to hurt her: They were like sisters. Her life now lies in the hands of the judge to decide her fate.

They took her handcuffs off from the hospital bed as they walked her through the outside double doors. She hasn't stopped crying ever since she found out what she'd done or thought she had done. She made her way to the car as the family followed. She took a ride in the police car straight to jail.

They stripped her naked and she changed into an orange jump suit to match the rest of her jail mates. Set at a million dollars, her bond was too expensive for her family to nearly afford. All she could do was wait for her assigned court date to arrive. The place was so unfamiliar to her: she was afraid. She cried every second she taught about what she did to land herself here, though she still didn't remember what truly happened that night. This was her first time in jail, and she knew she was properly never getting out because of the crime she was accused off; murder.

Her court date came with her parents praying for her freedom. On the other hand, Lisa's family prayed for her to be convicted for being a careless drunk driver that took the life of their loved one. They charged her as an adult since she was 16 and if she was found guilty, she would be charged with second degree murder since it was her first time ever getting in any kind of trouble.

"We the jury find Sia Singleton guilty of the murder of Lisa Joseph." She was shocked and speechless with a teary eye as they took her away. She glazed over at Lisa's husband who was carrying his newborn baby with one hand and holding on to his daughter with his other hand. He gave her an evil look as his eyes turned red. She knew right at that moment that her life was truly over. Her side of the family cried, while Lisa's side of the family rejoiced. They cried tears of joy for getting justice for her. David, Lisa's husband was motionless as they took Sia away. They gave her twenty-five to life sentencing with a chance of parole after 10 years.

She was in prison, terrified of her new life. She knew she couldn't show weakness while being in there, but she showed it anyway not knowing how to be strong yet. She was bullied, beaten, and sometimes would have her food taken from her. She would even starve herself most of the time and would only eat because she knew she had to survive somehow. She kept telling herself she didn't deserve to live.

The other inmates knew what they said she did, so they brought her misery for it.

Time starts to pass her by. She felt abandoned and lonely. She felt like they left her there to die in the arms of her cellmate, so she allowed the bullying to continue and never fought back. She thought she deserved every bit of it.

"People will always pick on you when you let them." Her new roommate said. She was her third cellmate since the other two almost beat her to death. She was the only one that treated her nicely. She felt bad for Sia regardless of what they said she had done. She was lost in a world that she was so unfamiliar with. She knew there was no way out, so she started to adjust and eventually started to fight back in some cases.

CHAPTER 11

David was trying so hard to adjust. Even with the help of his family and his dead wife's family, he was still struggling with his new life without his wife by his side. He had to learn how to care for a newborn baby on his own. He realized how much he didn't know about taking care of his children, including Amelia. He didn't know how to do her hair or pick out her outfit at first which made both of them frustrated. He didn't do a good job at preparing her for school. Lisa would do her hair and pick out her outfit, while David would rush to work every morning. The nanny was helpful, but he couldn't afford to pay her, so he had to let her go. His family stepped in to help when they could.

"I want mommy to do my hair."

"I can do it for now Amelia."

"No, you don't know how to daddy."

"But I'm trying. Please just be patient with me. I will be a master at it pretty soon sweetie…I promise." he joked, trying to brighten the conversation he was having with his daughter.

"But I want mom to do it."

"Sit down sweetie let me talk to you." David sat Amelia down on the bathroom vanity chair that he bought his wife Lisa for her Birthday last year. Lisa loved that chair and always sat there to do her makeup. Amelia also loves the chair and would always sit there to get her hair done before school by her mom.

"I know you want mommy back and I desperately want her back too, but she is not coming back."

"Why?" She asked.

"Because God called her up early to watch over us."

"But she was already doing that while she was here."

"She couldn't go everywhere with you, so God made her into this angel with the most beautiful wings you could only imagine. Now she can fly everywhere to protect you."

"But I don't see her." She said as he chuckled a little.

"She is an angel sweetie; you can't see her because angels are too beautiful and precious to be seen. You can only feel them and see them in your dreams."

"But I don't want her to be an angel, I want her to be my mommy." David fought back his tears before he continued.

"I am sorry baby, but she has to do what God says."

"Can you talk to God to bring her back?"

"I wish I could baby, but I think we should be happy for mommy because she is very happy right now. Don't you want her to be happy?"

"She was already happy with us."

"Yes, she was, but she is really happy now that she can watch over us more often."

"Ok!!" she said, still not satisfied.

"I got something for you."

"What?" he got up and went into Lisa's jewelry box and pulled out a 4-karat gold cross chain and placed it around her neck.

"Whenever you're missing her, just hold on to that chain really tight and she will be with you in spirit."

"Ok." She said with her hand on the cross of the chain over her neck.

CHAPTER 12

Just when Sia thought she was getting used to her new normal life, she got an unexpected guest. She didn't know who it was at first; until she walked in the visitor's room where you can only talk to your guest through the phone. She saw him and immediately froze. She didn't know if she should walk away or sit down to talk. The only thing she could remember from him was the look he gave her when she last saw him. She sat down and took a deep breath before grabbing the phone to face him.

"I know I'm the last person you were expecting to see." David said with a frown.

"It's ok."

"No, it's not ok; if you hadn't killed my wife with your carelessness, we wouldn't be here."

"I'm sorry...I truly am." Sia said.

"Sorry will never bring my wife back so you can stop saying that!" David tried to control his frustration as one of the officers looked in their direction. Sia kept quiet, afraid to speak another word that would provoke him.

"You know what? I came here to see you face to face and just say that I forgive you, but I just can't seem to do that after what I have gone through every single fucking day. I have to explain to my little girl every time why her mother is never coming home!" He said, then continued "Do you know how hard that has been for me? Knowing she doesn't fully understand still? All she wants is for me to make her mother come home. I can't give her that all because of you and your careless mistakes." Sia was still quiet with guilt as he continued. "So no, I don't know how I can forgive you." She sobbed feeling so guilty and disappointed of what she had become 'a murderer'

"No matter how long you will sit here and rot, it wouldn't bring my wife back." He said as she cried even more as she sat there with the phone in her ears, afraid to speak a word. He dropped the phone and walked away. He then rushed back with anger feeling unsatisfied as he banged on the glass window right in front of her face. "I HOPE YOU DIE IN HERE FOR RUINING MY LIFE!!" He screamed as Sia jumped back. The guard rushed to him to hold him back. He snatched himself away from him and walked away as he wiped the tears off his face, with anger still brewing in his chest.

CHAPTER 13

"We can't keep living like nothing happened Allen." Davina said while lying next to him.

"What now?" He was irritated and showed it through a frown.

"Sia is still in jail for something she didn't do."

"Is that the story you've been telling people?"

"No, of course not."

"Then what's the problem?"

"She's my best friend."

"So, you want me to go turn myself in?"

"No…I mean I don't know" she said. He got on top of her and dripped his firm manly hands tight around her neck.

"Allen…You're hurting me." she said gasping for air.

"Am I?" he squeezed tighter.

"Please stop" she said, coughing at this point.

"Should I?"

"Yes please… I… swear I won't tell a soul."

"I don't know if I can trust you anymore."

"You can. I swear you can… Please!" her face started turning purple and red.

"I don't want to hear about this Sia girl ever again you hear me?"

"Yes… yes!" she said as he loosened his grip. She laid there afraid to say another word while he laid next to her like he didn't almost just kill her. She went home that night fearing for her life; she just knew either way she was going to lose at the end of all this.

CHAPTER 14

Davina laid in her bed restless, wondering how she ended up with a man she is now afraid of.

She met him eight months ago when she was out running as usual. She was running back home when Allen almost ran her over.

"Hey! Watch where you're going."

"I'm sorry, I wasn't paying attention."

"I can see that!" she said, angry that she almost got ran over.

"Sorry...I'll pay better attention next time." He gazed at her up and down, admiring her beauty from head to toe.

"I hope so." She had a much softer tone now that she realized he had lust in his eyes for her.

"I'm Allen." He said as he passed her an introductory handshake with ease.

"Davina!" she shook his hand.

"Pleasure to meet you...Davina."

"Likewise, though you almost just killed me." she said as he chuckled.

"If you keep reminding me about that, I may just have to take you out to show you how sorry I really am." He said with a smile, admiring how attractive she was. Allen just got out of jail and wanted a companion. By the look on her face, he knew he found the one.

"Hmm where did you come from by the way? I haven't seen you around here before." She asked.

"So... you know everyone in this neighborhood?" he laughed.

"Uh…Pretty much" she said confidently.

"Well, I'm not from this area, but i hope that doesn't mean "no" to going out with you."

"Okay then…Allen," she said with a slight pause in between her words. "It better be worth almost losing my life for today!" she joked with a blush, liking what was in front of her.

He laughed "pretty much, what better way can I make up for my carelessness?"

CHAPTER 15

Allen was right on time in her life. She was going through a lot; her and her family were struggling to cope with what happened to her twin brother. It got harder and harder every day that passes by before Allen came into the picture. He was so attractive and treated her good; this made Davina feel so much better.

Davina had a twin brother Devon who lost his life in the streets. He was at the wrong place at the wrong time, or so they thought. Him and Davina were always so close. They used to do everything together until they went to high school. He got mixed up with the wrong crowd which eventually took him to a place of no return. A place that he enjoyed more than anywhere or anything. He would always get high and steal with them even when he knew he had access to all the money he could ever dreamed of. He even stole from his own parents even though he had access to anything he wanted. They just couldn't understand why he would do that when he can easily ask for anything. Their family was wealthy with his father being a successful lawyer and their mom being a doctor.

He kept going down the wrong path and anything they tried to do to help him just kept backfiring. They didn't know what else to do so they prayed that he would change before it was too late.

One day Davina asked him "what are you doing?"

"What do you mean?" he replied.

"Why are you doing this to yourself?"

"What am I doing?" he said with a giggle.

"You are high right now, aren't you?"

"What are you talking about?" He tried to act clueless.

"You're just throwing your life away like it means nothing to you."

"Come on Davina, I'm just living my life."

"Getting high and hanging with the wrong people is not living, it's being stupid."

"J-e-s-u-s! You worry too much sis. I'm fine, trust me I am…now can you let this go?"

"Give me a reason not to worry then. Stop smoking and stop hanging around with those people."

"So now you're trying to control me like mom and dad?"

"No, I'm trying to save your life!"

"From what?" He looked at Davina like she had no clue what she was talking about.

"You are constantly high and spending most of your time with these boys and missing school so much that they kicked you out."

"Man, fuck school, it's over-rated."

"What do you mean fuck school? You sound so stupid right now I wish you could hear yourself."

"I can hear myself and I sound brilliant!" He said in sarcasm with a smile on his face.

"What if something happens to you out there?" She said scared for her brother's life.

"Relax mom…" he mocked "aren't nothing going to happen to me, I'm ok…promise."

"But you don't know that for sure."

"I do know that because I aren't out there slipping up. I'm always on top of my shit."

"But you don't even have to live like this, you're just a sophomore and already got kicked out of school."

"School just aren't for me sis!"

"Then what is for you?"

"Freedom. I just want to be free to live how I want, without any-body breathing down my fucking back."

"Mom and dad just want to protect you, not take your freedom from you."

"Man whatever, can we cut this short? You're fucking up my high." He laughed, meanwhile Davina still had on a serious face. She was hoping to get through to him before it's too late.

"What happened to you Devon? You've completely changed."

"Wow… didn't I say drop it? What is it Davina? You wanted me to stay a kid forever?"

"No, I wanted you to be the fun normal brother like you used to be."

"I am!"

"You are far from it right now!"

"Man whatever…we all grow up someday and I'm tired of the kiddy shit anyways." He said brushing her off.

"Please get it together, you are only 14."

"I'm fine, like I said before!" He turned the other way with a grin on his face. He was too high and wasn't too concerned about what Davina was saying.

He was so high off life and confident to the point that he thought nothing could touch him. He left one day and told Davina he would be back. That day, Davina felt something wasn't right; she knew she couldn't stop him either, so she ignored the knot that was digging in her stomach and went upstairs to her room to do her homework.

She finished her homework and Devon still wasn't back, but this was usually normal for him these days. On that particular day, she felt different; she felt uneasy and just wanted him to walk through the door any moment so she could feel peace in her heart. She went downstairs to the kitchen where her mom was cooking dinner.

 "Hey mom!" Davina greeted as she entered the kitchen.

"Hey darling, you finished your homework?"

"Sure did!"

"Good. Where's your brother?" she asked while stirring the food in the pot.

"I don't know..."

"He's not upstairs?"

"No!"

"He went out?"

"Yeah."

"Did he tell you where he was going?"

"He never does."

"I don't know what's wrong with that boy. He doesn't get that senseless behavior from me. I really hope he gets it together."

"Me too."

"Maybe moving away from this city to new scenery will help."

"But I don't want to move, I like my school."

"I know sweetie, but it's not working for your brother."

"What about me? I want to stay."

"Don't you want your brother to get better?"

"Yes, but we don't have to move because of him..."

"Well, maybe not. It's just a thought." Mrs. Martin said as Davina frowned her face, knowing her parents will do whatever it takes to save their son's life.

The day was fading away fast with no sign of Devon. The parents did not worry too much at first knowing this was how things were lately. He always found his way back home late at night when they were all asleep. They have tried everything to make him follow the rules, but discipline just didn't work out for him. They would put him on punishment and ground him, but he still managed to get away with leaving whenever he pleased. They even kicked him out of the house and Mrs. Martin would always worry and go find him. That made it worse because he knew they would always come look for him to come back home. That day after dinner, Davina and her parents sat in the living room and watched a movie. After the movie was over, they sat in an awkward silence with Devan on their mind, knowing it was getting darker by the second.

The doorbell rang and everyone's attention turned to the door.

"Who could that be?" their father said.

"I don't know, but Devon has a key." Mrs. Martin responded.

"Yeah...Unless he lost it!" Davina said.

"That's Possible," their father said.

"Davina, go see who is at the door please!" their mother Elizabeth commanded politely.

"Okay," she walked up to the door and asked, "who is it?"

"It's Officer Robert, from the Police Department" she was shocked to know an officer was at their doorstep.

"Mom..., Dad..., a police officer is at the door!" she whispered. Davina knew her brother was probably in trouble again. Her hands started to sweat like they usually do when she gets bad news about him. They both got up quickly to meet her at the door. Davina's father opened the door.

"How may I help you officer?" he was confused and just wanted to know what was wrong.

"Yes, I tracked Mr. Devon Martin back to this address; do you happen to know him?"

"Yes of course…. that's my son. Is he in trouble or something?" Mrs. Martin came closer to the officer.

"What's going on with our son?" She asked Officer Robert.

"May I come in Sir…Ma'am?" he said looking at both of them as Davina stood at the back of her parents. Officer Robert was trying to find a way to tell the Martin family what happened to Devon. Even years of experience doing this, he still struggled with telling families horrible news about their relatives.

"You can tell us what's going on here, did he get arrested again for stealing?" Mr. Martin started guessing, started to feel impatient with the officer.

"No sir I'm sorry to say this, but we found your son's body and I'm afraid he is no longer with us." Everyone stood there frozen, unable to process what the officer said fast enough.

Mrs. Martin started crying out to the top of her lungs; she could not possibly believe what she was hearing.

"You said what?" Mr. Martin finally spoke with a shaky voice.

"I'm truly sorry for your loss."

"No no no no no no no it can't be, it's not possible!" Mrs. Martin said, unable to control her tears. Davina stood there frozen; she couldn't believe what she was hearing either. She just knew deep down in her heart it was a very bad dream that she was about to wake up from.

"You must've gotten the wrong person because my son is still alive, he can't be dead!" Mrs. Martin said, trying to convince herself and the officer that they got the wrong person as she shook in fear that it may also be true.

"I understand how you may be feeling, but this is the wallet we saw in his pocket which identified him." He gave them the wallet which their nightmare comes to life.

"I need to see the body now!" Mrs. Martin ran outside as if the officer must've brought the body with him.

"He was rushed to the hospital where they pronounced him dead." The office said as he followed behind.

"What hospital?" she said shaking out of control.

"St Mary's Hospital." She rushed to grab her bag and key, while crying uncontrollably.

They all rushed to the hospital as fast as they could; the entire ride was like no other. They got to the hospital as the nurse took them to go see the body in the morgue to confirm if it was really Devon.

Mrs. Martin broke down again, she just couldn't control herself. She held on to her son's dead body and they all cried together.

CHAPTER 16

They went home that night and sat in the living room. It was so quiet, and everyone looked like zombies from the crying and confusion. Davina just lost her twin and only sibling in the world; meanwhile their parents just lost their only son who they felt they could've saved, had they moved to a better place. They knew his friends and lifestyle would be his fate if they stayed there any longer; now it was too late.

People started stopping by that night to be there for them after the news spread. They were really devastated by what just happened. Their dad was so angry and just wanted to find who had killed their son. Mrs. Martin was devastated for not being able to protect him from the choices that ended his life. Davina was just mute and couldn't stop crying. Their lives changed that night, even with all the money they had in the world; they couldn't save him.

The detective that investigated the crime still couldn't find a lead. A few people knew what happened, but no one was stepping up to tell the detective who did it. They were afraid for their own safety. The case went cold, which brought no peace to the family knowing his killer was still out there.

On the day of the funeral, the church service was filled with love and compassion. They brought his body to the cemetery where the family waited to have their son buried. As they reeled him into the deep six-foot hole in the ground, Davina spotted a car that pulled up on the sidewalk. She couldn't help but to notice something was off with the two people in that car. A girl in the front seat looked sad and guilty like she knew something. The driver appeared to have an awkward frown on his face. They drove off, but Davina quickly memorized the plate number. Davina's mom was crying as she watched her son get put in the ground. Davina quickly whispered in her mom's ear and asked for a pen. "Mom, I need a pen…quick." Her mother looked at her with confusion, not understanding what she was trying to do. "I need to write something down…hurry before I forget it."

"Davina, they are putting your brother down and you want a pen?" she said with irritation with tears still in her eyes.

"Yes, I think I saw who may be responsible for his death." Everyone looked at them confused at what they were doing during a time like this.

"Who?" She asked.

Devon's coffin rested at the bottom of the ground.

"Just give me a pen before I forget!" she quickly reached in her purse to look for a pen. Her hands were shaking so much she was having trouble finding one. She couldn't find one so she pulled out her phone "Here, I can't find a pen, write it here!"

Davina grabbed the phone and wrote down the plate number she had memorized in her head.

"What did you just write down?" her mom asked.

"A plate numbers. I'll tell you about later."

Mr. Martin looked disappointed that they were being disruptive at the end of their son's funeral.

They brought their focus back on the funeral right on time, as they were about to cover him with dirt. Everyone placed their roses into the grave and said their goodbyes. The Martins stood behind for everyone to leave. "What was that all about?" their father said, facing both of them.

"I think I saw the person that was responsible for this."

"Where?" Mr. Martin said, giving her the same reaction, her

mother did.

"They were parked on the sidewalk and I memorized their plate number while they drove off. That was why I went to mom so I could write it down before I forgot."

"Ok good, we need to take this to the detective now."

"It's Saturday, he may not be there." Davina said.

"Then let's call first to see if he is there. They called and somebody else picked up the phone.

"This is officer Richard."

"Hello, I was calling to see if Officer Raymond was available."

"What is this in regard to?" he asked.

"We may have a lead about the murder of my son Devon Martin."

"Ok, let me take your number down and have him call you back."

"Ok thank you." he gave the officer his number then disconnected the call.

"So, I guess we can go home now and just wait for him to call us back," Mr. Martin said to both of them.

They were just walking in the door of their home when they got a call.

"Hello, this is Darnel Martin." Their father answered his phone.

"Hello Mr. Martin, this is Officer Raymond. I heard you have some information regarding who may be involved in your son's death?"

"Yes, I think we do. My daughter saw a car that looked suspicious at my son's funeral today. She took down the license plate number while they were parked at the sidewalk, watching for a while."

"Oh great, I can meet you guys at the station in an hour if you are available."

"Yes, we can. We can be on our way there now!"

"Ok great, see you in a few." They were at the station in 15 minutes and waited until he got there.

 "So, he was driving in a navy-blue BMW?" he repeated and kept writing as Davina gave the information she had collected.

"Yes."

"Did you get a good look at the driver?"

"No, I just knew a guy was driving and a girl was in the passenger side."

"Ok, well we should be able to track down who owns the vehicle with the license plate number you got; then we can just go from there."

"Thank you." Elizabeth, their mother said.

"No problem. I just hope we catch the killer soon, to give you and your family some sort of peace and justice."

"We hope so too!" Darnel, their father said.

"Do you know around the time you saw him there at the funeral?"

"I'm not sure, it was around maybe 2:30pm when we were putting my brother into the ground." Her heart skipped a bit with pain, as she altered those words.

"Ok, that was really helpful. We will start on this right away and keep you guys informed on what we found. We will also look around the area to see if any surveillance camera caught the face of the driver. But overall, we have enough information to hopefully fish out the killer and bring whoever it is forward."

"Thank you so much officer Raymond, we are very grateful." Darnel got up and shook his hand.

"No problem, anything that I can do to help. We will try our best to get the killer off the streets before they strike again." The officer said.

"Thank you, we really appreciate it." Their mother responded.

CHAPTER 17

They went their separate ways in the house when they got back home. Their mother went to Devon's room and laid in the bed holding onto a piece of the artwork he created a few weeks before he died. He wanted to become an artist one day.

"In order for you to become a great artist, you will have to stay focused, keep practicing and stay off the streets." Elizabeth said to him a few weeks before he died.

"But I'm already great at it, I don't need to keep practicing." He Bragged.

"That's not what all the greatest artists of all time said, they've always said something about focusing and practicing."

"They must not have been that great then, to still be practicing."

"Well, the world thinks otherwise because they are famous now."

"Hmmm that's good to know, because now I can tell the world when the time comes that I become a great artist without much practice; I was born with the talent." He bragged with a smirk on his face.

Elizabeth cried as she was going down memory lane of what he could've become. She cried every day; barely ate, rarely showered, and barely came out of that room for anything. She wasn't ready to let go.

Darnel had to step up and became the strong one for them both. He didn't push too hard for them to take a bath or leave the room; he was only making sure they ate to stay alive. He was grieving also and was barely doing those things himself. Every flashback of his son brought tears to his eyes. He remembered when he was trying to talk him out of being an artist to play ball.

"Dad I don't want to play ball; I want to become an artist."

"Look at you, you are built like a ballplayer, just try it and see how you like it."

"Ok so what if I try it and don't like it, then what?"

"Then I won't ask anymore. But all I'm asking from you right now is when you do try it, be open to it to fully get the fill of it before making a decision."

"Deal!!" he said with a smile, knowing his mind was already made up before he even tried it.

CHAPTER 18

The detectives went through the leads they had, and it led them to Justin Lee. They presented his picture to Davina, but she could not fully identify him. She said it may be the guy since she didn't fully see his face. But that was not enough evidence to arrest him. They kept digging until they found the girl that was with him that day. Davina knew that was the girl that was sitting on the passenger's side of the suspicious car. They found her and brought her in and kept pushing for answers until she finally cracked.

"I didn't know it would end up like this." she broke down.

"What would end up like this?" Detective Raymond asked.

"I didn't know he was going to kill him."

"Why did he kill him?"

"Because he thought we were messing around. I could've prevented this whole thing if I just told him the truth."

"What truth?"

"That we never messed around."

"Ok, so let's start from the beginning," the detective said then continued "what happened that led to the death of Devon?"

"Justin thought I was messing with Devon, which wasn't true. I didn't tell him it wasn't true because I was upset at the fact that he cheated on me. I just wanted him to hurt like I did, but not to hurt anybody else over it."

"So, what made him think in the first place that Devon was messing with you? Did he see you guys together, or did you just tell him that you were messing with him when you weren't."

"Both."

"And then what?"

"When he saw him again, they got into an argument; I didn't think it was going to get past that." She said as she continued to sob.

"But it did and now Devon is dead!" The head detective said with frustration.

"I am so sorry; I swear I didn't mean for that to happen."

"I'm sure you didn't, but he still died for it." She cried as the detective left her in the room to talk about what to do with her.

"She is as guilty as he is because she is the real reason he is dead. She could've prevented all of this, but she didn't; all because she wanted to make her boyfriend jealous."

"So, we are charging her?"

"Absolutely..." They went back in the room and put her in handcuffs then took her away. Justin knew they were looking for him at this point, so he fled. It took over a month before they could track him down a thousand miles away.

CHAPTER 19

Davina and her family felt relieved when they brought Devon's killer to justice, but they still weren't at peace. They would've preferred him to get the death sentence since they couldn't get their son back. Later, they packed all their belongings and moved away to a different state. They moved to Washington where they had family, but Davina hated it. She didn't want to move in the first place, even after her brother died. She already lost him and now she didn't want to lose her friends too.

She felt like she had to start all over again, but this time it was different. She wasn't the happy girl they all knew. She was the new girl in town, and she was angry with an attitude. She would lash out at home and in school and was ready to fight over any little thing that rubbed her the wrong way. Their parents were even more hurt that their move had affected their only child left. They didn't know what else to do. They fought and attacked each other until it led to them getting a divorce. With Davina's parents being divorced, it ruined her even more. She felt like she was losing everything and the only person she could always turn to, was her friend Sia. Her and Sia became friends when they had a project to do together. They got along well, although they were two different people with different personalities. Sia was more levelheaded, meanwhile Davina was more of the outspoken one. They kind of balanced each other out and where inseparable.

At first Nita, Sia's friend since elementary school, wasn't too fond of Davina. She later grew to tolerate her for the sake of Sia, but Nita didn't hang out with them as much as she used to with just Sia. They still spoke every now and then, but not as much as it used to be. Regardless of what happened, Nita was always there

NILEYAH MARY ROSE

for Sia no matter what.

CHAPTER 20

Nita walked through the double door to the prison cell. She went through security and did the required processes before waiting to sit down with Sia.

"Hey!" Nita said when she sat down and picked up the phone.

"Hey!" Sia said flatly.

"How are you?"

"Can't complain really."

"How are you holding up?"

"I don't even know, but I'm adjusting." She spoke. She took a breath then continued to speak "I'm just trying to program myself to get used to spending the rest of my life in here."

"Yeah, I've been meaning to come see you, because I've been so confused about this."

"What?" Sia said nonchalantly.

"How were you driving that night when Davina told me you weren't going to be driving?"

"She did?"

"Yes, she said you were too drunk to drive, which you clearly were."

"Well clearly, I don't remember. So, she told you I wasn't going to be driving?"

"Yes, she did. She was literally pulling you out of there and then she said she wouldn't risk her life with you driving her."

"I guess she still let me drive anyway, because I was in front of the wheel."

"Or maybe someone else was driving and they didn't want the person to take the blame for it. How I see it… it was easier to put the owner of the car in front of the wheel after the fact."

She laughed then responded, "That doesn't even make any sense, Davina wouldn't do that to me."

"She wouldn't? Not even for her boyfriend maybe? Sia, you were so drunk you could barely stand on your feet. The rest of them were pretty ok to walk."

"But she's my best friend, she wouldn't do that to me."

"And that is her boyfriend and we both know she will do anything for him." Sia's eyes got wider.

"What are you saying to me?"

"You know what I'm saying. Can't you see the way she's been acting? She is guilty of something and you know that deep down."

"It can't be, you just want somebody to take the blame for my action."

"No, I just want justice for you."

"Davina wouldn't do this to me, she is one of my best friends."

"Ok, whatever you say. Just be open minded about that night. Who would let a passed out drunk person drive them? Especially when they were sober…"

"Do you think…?"

"I don't know. I'm just saying. Have your lawyer look into things."

"Things like what exactly?"

"I don't know, street camera or whatever. All you need to know is who was really driving that car. Don't you at least want to know?"

"What if it was me though?"

"Then you'll know for sure. Don't you want clarity since you didn't see what happened?"

"I do…"

"Ok then, find out!"

"Alright then I will; but the thing is, my lawyer is Davina's dad."

"Get another one if you think he won't be honest about what he finds out."

"No, it's not that…I mean, he has been good to me."

"But that's Davina's dad," she said then continued "maybe you should use another lawyer if you don't think he may be truthful to you."

"I don't think he would lie to me about it. Besides, he was free."

"Well see if he can find a tape of anything about who was driving that night. If not, get another lawyer."

"Ok. Thank you!"

"You're welcome. Well, I got to go now, but 'I'll be back later to check on you."

"Ok. Thanks!" Sia spent the entire night pacing back and forth, wondering if Nita could be right.

"Vina wouldn't do that to me." She said as she kept beating herself up about it repeatedly. She couldn't even process it in her head, that she could slightly be innocent based on what Nita just told her. She just knew deep down in her heart that Davina wouldn't betray her like that. A part of her was hoping Nita was right.

CHAPTER 21

Day after day, she pondered about it; even when Davina came to visit her a month later.

 "What's wrong? Davina asked, noticing that something was on her mind."

"Nothing really."

"It looks like something is bothering you!

"There kind of is something bothering me, but I don't know how to bring it up."

"Talk to me, we are still BFFs remember?"

"I know, that's why what I have in mind wouldn't make sense."

"What is it?"

"About the night of the accident, I know you were passed out in the car too. Do you think maybe when the accident happened, that one of the boys moved me in the driver's seat to take the blame since it was my car anyway?" Davina's heart skipped a beat.

"Why would you say that?" she said frightened inside with her face frowned as she began to sweat.

Sia sighed "I don't know... I just want clarity from that night."

"Sia, you were driving drunk and you are already in here paying for that. Just let it go..." She said with frustration.

"I know, but a part of me just wanted to know after speaking with Nita."

"I see... So, she is the one in here feeding you hopes and dreams?"

"She's just trying to help because she said I was really drunk that night. So, lighten up Vina, I was just saying."

"You were the one driving and I was in the car with you remember?"

"Yes, according to what you told me. But you were passed out too, remember?"

"You're right but we were already on the road before I fell asleep."

"Ok. Well, I don't know, I just feel like I need to do something before I completely give up."

"Well how would you find out who was driving then?"

"I don't know, there's got to be a camera somewhere that captured something."

"Sia, believe me when I say you were driving. Now let it go!" she said as she slammed the phone and left. Sia felt bad for bringing it up after seeing her reaction. She didn't want to lose her over this, so she decided to let it go and forget about the possibility of being innocent.

CHAPTER 22

Davina went straight to Allen's house right after to tell him what had happened. "That Nita bitch is running her mouth." Allen opened the door as she walked in panicking.

"What are you talking about now baby?" he closed the door behind them before facing her.

"She told Sia to go look at cameras from that night of the accident." She said as they stood face to face to each other.

"What cameras?"

"Any street cameras, I don't know."

"Why would she tell her that?" He said with a little agitation.

"Because she is trying to convince her she didn't do it."

"Where will she get that idea from huh?" Allen said moving closer to Davina as she moved back a little, frightened at the frown on his face. He was exasperated thinking Davina had said something out of guilt.

"I don't know, I don't even talk to her..." she said defensively.

"When was the last time you saw her?"

"Few months ago, at the store."

"So, you didn't tell her anything?"

"Are you serious right now?" She said now feeling annoyance that he would question her loyalty.

"Yes I am. What did you tell her?" he said with a poker face.

"Are you seriously questioning me? After everything we've been through together?”

“Yes. You know ya females can get emotional and open ya mouth.”

“So, you're telling me you don't trust me!”

“I don't know. Should I?”

“When have I gone against you?”

“Again, I don't know. Where would she get the idea from suddenly to see who was actually driving that night huh?”

“I don't know Allen, I really don't.”

“Ok. Well, I will take care of it then” He said while walking away from her to the kitchen.

“How?” she walked behind him.

“You don't worry about that, just try to keep your mouth shut and control your damn emotions.”

“My emotions are controlled. But how are you going to take care of it?”

“Didn't I say don't worry? But… you can do me one favor though…” He turned around to face her again.

“What would that be?”

“Get that girl's address for me.”

“Why?” She responded with apprehension.

“You ask too many damn questions. Just trust me I will take care of it!” he said while pulling on her cheek softly with a smirk on his face.

“Allen don't do nothing stupid!” she warned him with panic, knowing what he was capable of.

“I wouldn't, I just want to chat with her.”

“About what?” she questioned him.

"Don't worry about it, just trust me and get me her damn address..." He said feeling short tempered with her.

"No, I don't feel comfortable doing that."

"So, you don't trust me?"

"I do, but..."

"But what?" he paused and continued "look, everything is going to be ok. I just need to chat with her to convince her to keep her mouth shut." She didn't respond, not knowing what to say.

Don't you still want to be with me?" He said with a little bit of a sweet tone.

"I do!"

"Then act like it and get me her information." He said and then used his right hand to pull her face closer to his softly. "If I don't talk to her, she may find a way to convince the 'Sia' girl that she is innocent. We can't get sloppy now." He kept his voice sweet and tender; he found it best this way to get his point across. She was right about his motives, but he had to hide it to keep things from getting sloppier.

"But my dad is a lawyer, I can talk to him!"

"What are you going to tell him huh? You know he doesn't like me." He said as he took a deep breath with irritation.

"Ok fine! How about I call her and plan to meet her somewhere; to try to talk some sense into her maybe?"

"Ok cool, then I'll take it from there." He went to the fridge to grab a drink.

"How are you planning to do this? Just tell me already!!" at this point she was aggravated.

"Nothing... Just meet her wherever you decide, then I will step in if she doesn't listen to you."

"What exactly are your plans if she doesn't listen to me?"

"Damn you ask a lot of questions!" He said as he chuckled

"I wouldn't if you'd just tell me something."

"You don't have to know everything. It's safer for you this way if anything does happen. Just know your man will take care of it if you can't." He kissed her on her lips. She was not comfortable about the plan, but she knew she couldn't disappoint him.

Davina placed a call in front of Allen who was watching.

"Hello" Nita said while picking up.

"Hey Nita, it's Davina."

"Oh hey." She uttered in confusion. She didn't understand why she was getting a call from Davina suddenly.

"What are you up to?"

"Nothing…why?"

 "Oh, it's nothing really, it's just that I haven't spoken to you in a while and I was just seeing if you want to meet for a coffee or something later?"

"For what?" Nita was shortcoming, she didn't trust her.

"Oh nothing, you know I haven't really been out ever since Sia went to jail and I kind of want to reconnect with people."

"Oh." She replied with a dry response.

"So, do you mind meeting me for coffee? I really just want to talk to somebody."

"Sure, when?" She said opening up a little bit.

"Hmm how about…" she looked at Allen who worded out tomorrow "tomorrow?"

"Sure, what time?"

"Hum…" he looked at Allen again who mouthed out another word that she couldn't understand to repeat "I can text you the time if you don't mind!"

"Sure." Nita hung up.

"So now what?"

"Call her back and tell her to meet you at the Global Coffee at 7pm."

"I can just text her that instead of calling her again."

"You can't just text her, that'll leave a direct form of evidence."

"For what? What is your plans Allen? I hope you're not planning to do anything stupid to her."

"Watch your mouth and do as I say!" he was getting aggravated by her questioning him.

"No, not until you tell me what your plans are." she said with her hands gripped on her hips.

"You're going to have to trust me on this one baby!" he said while walking off to the bedroom.

"I'm really trying Allen, but you don't tell me anything."

"You will find out soon enough, just tell her the time and place" Davina was hesitant. "Don't worry, everything will be alright after I talk to her." She took a deep breath then called again to do as instructed.

CHAPTER 23

Davina went home that day leaving Allen feeling concerned. He did not like the way she has been acting fragile ever since the accident. Davina's strong personality was what drew her to him and now it seems as if things had altered; she was becoming to remind him of his mother Maria lately and he hated it.

Allen's relationship with his mother was not as good as it used to be, life was good for him at first, until his father lost his job and couldn't support the family anymore. He turned to alcohol to numb the shame he was feeling, which led him to become violent towards his wife. Allen was powerless when his father would beat on his mother. He hated the fact that she was weak and fragile towards his abuse and he could not understand why. He told himself he would never fall for a woman that showed any signs of weakness, but it seems like his promises to himself had failed when he met the other side of Davina after the accident.

Allen remembered when his father would beat on his mother like a bag of shit, as if she deserved it. He used to hate him for putting his hands on her but hated her more for letting it happen. Maria would fight back sometimes when it got too bad; she would always lose. But she never dared to call the police on him. Allen tried doing it for her one day when he beat her senselessly and left her swollen and bloody.

'911 what's your emergency?" Allen called the police to put a stop to the abuse once and for all, He also wanted to save his own sanity from seeing the abuse happen on repeat. It killed him to always watch his mother fight for her life, but could do nothing about it.

"I would like to report my dad for beating up my mom." Ten-year-old Allen said on the phone, with tears pouring down his eyes.
"Allen who are you talking to?" Maria leaped her way to him as fast as she could with panic, when she heard him talking on the phone about her abuse; she didn't want anybody to know.
"The police mama!" she quickly grabbed the phone from his hand to fix his mess again; this was the second time Allen is calling the police on his father.
"Hello! sorry don't listen to my son; me and his father were just playing... It's nothing really." He stood aside with his face fully frowned; he was hot in rage along with his hands folded, knowing she was lying her ass off.

"Are you sure? because the little child sounded concerned on the phone."
"I'm sure. It's not his fault, he didn't see what happened."
"So there is no violence going on in your household?"
"No violence whatsoever. My son just thought me, and his father were fighting, but that wasn't the case."

He wanted to scream 'she is lying!!!' but he knew better after seeing the way she looked at him through her swollen bloody face. He didn't want her to take her frustration out on him, so he stood aside with resentment on how stupid she was over a man who sold her ring while she was asleep; to satisfy his drinking habit. *You don't need a ring; you already have me.* He said to her when she found out what he did to her wedding ring.
"Is there a reason he would believe you two weren't playing? Has something violent ever happened before?"
"Dammit no, I just told you what happened and nothing violent ever happens in this house alright? My son just misunderstood." she said with frustration and hung up.
"Boy is you out of your fucking mind?" She yelled at him.
"No you are!!" He said as his words backfired; she leaned over to him and slapped him with rage.

"I take enough shit from your dad just to keep this family together; I don't need extra shit from you alright!!" She said to Allen with anger in her tone. She was hurt and angry at the same time. She was tired of the abuse, but she just didn't know how to get out or start over. Besides, she hadn't worked for years ever since they got married.

"But I don't want us all together, he keeps hurting you."

"I'm ok. Don't worry about me." She said with a softer tone as she leaned towards him. "Your dad is sick right now; he needs help, and we can't leave him."

"He is a drunk."

"Watch how you talk about your father."

"But he is!!"

"What the fuck did I say?"

She said then walked off to clean herself off before her husband came home; he would come back after the liquor cleared from his eyes to beg for mercy once again. Allen became numb to it all.

CHAPTER 24

Davina sat at the Global Coffee shop waiting patiently for Nita. All she could think of while sitting there, was what could Allen possibly be up to. "This fucker better not does anything stupid." She said as she thought about how much trouble Allen is. She was hoping she didn't show up, but minutes later someone tapped her on the shoulder. "Oh shit... you scared me." Davina jumped hesitantly.

"I'm sorry!"

"It's ok." she said as Nita took a seat in front of her.

"It looks like you were deep in thought." Nita said while seated.

"Oh really?"

"Yes, because I walked right up to you and you didn't budge." She said half smiling, knowing something was heavy on her mind

"Sorry... just a lot on my mind."

"Talk to me, what's going on?"

"Nothing really, just still bothered about my friend being in jail."

"Are you really?" She said, giving her the side eye.

"Of course, why would you say that?" Davina nervously asked.

"Oh, it's nothing, I'm just making sure."

"You wouldn't just say that if it wasn't something. What did you hear?"

"Nothing..."

"Mm, well I heard you went to go see Sia the other day." Davina said trying to get her to talk about the conversation she had with Sia.

"How would you know about that?"

"Come on Nita, that's still my friend; we still talk about things."

"So, she told you about my reasons for being concerned?"

"What reasons...What concerns?"

"That she may not have been the person driving that night.

"Where would you even get that idea from?"

"You!!"

"Me?" she responded in shock.

"Yes…you."

"When did I tell you that??"

"The same night. You told me she was too drunk to drive."

"But that's her car Nita; I couldn't stop her from driving if she kept pushing."

"You could have. You also said over your dead body she was not driving you anywhere."

"Well, she did."

"Did she really?" She gave her the side eye again.

"What is that supposed to mean?" she said with frustration as her heartbeat with fear.

"Nothing, I'm just saying; she may not have been the driver that night."

"Then who?"

"You tell me!"

"Look, you sound delusional right now. Sia was driving and that's that." Davina said, getting even more frustrated.

"If you say so, but honestly I'm not buying it."

"Ok detective Nita, think what you want... but I know I would never do anything to hurt my best friend."

"Is that what you're saying to yourself?"

"What is your problem?"

"I don't think you are telling the truth."

"What is the truth then, since you happen to know so much."

"I was hoping you would tell me."

"I told you the fucking truth!"

"I know you well enough Davina."

"No, you don't."

"Ok whatever... from what I know, you wouldn't let anybody just drive you home while they were that drunk. You never have, and you never will period."

"But she did though."

"And I don't believe it."

"Ok whatever, believe you want; I'm done with this conversation." Davina walked out furiously. She was also nervous knowing she couldn't get through to her.

"She's not budging!!" she said when she got Allen on the phone.

"I will take care of it then."

"What are you going to do?"

"Don't worry, I will get through to her."

"And if you don't?" Allen hung up without answering her question.

"This fucker!!" she said as she slammed her phone down and drove home with her heart racing uncontrollably. Meanwhile, Nita was driving home on a misty road as a car pulled in front of her. She freaked out and stepped on the brakes hard. She saw Allen coming out of his car with a straight face. "What's your problem?" Nita asked with confusion.

"I should be asking you that." He said while walking up to her with a gun in his back pocket.

"You're the one that got in front of me like a damn maniac." She said, as he frowned his face at her comment. He then quickly loosened up his frown to place a smile on his face to keep her at ease. But Nita knew better, so she stayed on edge.

"What do you know about that night?"

"Oh, I see Davina sent you over here since she couldn't convince me with her lies."

"It wasn't a lie, the Sia girl was driving." He said, losing his patient.

"No way... She was too drunk to be driving, so no I don't buy it from you either."

"Have you gone to the police yet?"

"Not yet!"

"Good..." he said then quickly pulled the gun from his back pocket. Without hesitation, he shot her in the head twice and checked her pulse to make sure she was dead before fleeing the scene.

CHAPTER 25

A week later, the officer was at Davina's front door.

"Can I help you, officer?" Davina said with a panic tone. She felt that Nita may have said something to the police by now.

"Yes. My name is detective Owen...do you have a moment to talk?" he said as he cleared his throat.

"I think so." her nerves were out of control.

"Ok good, I would like for you to come down to the station with me for some quick questions."

"About what?"

"I'll let you know when we get there."

"Ok" she said confused, but also scared knowing something had happened. She panicked all the way to the station.

"When did you last see your friend Nita?" her heart skipped a bit when he said her name.

"I don't remember, it's been a little while ago."

"Are you sure about that?"

"Yeah why?"

"Well according to the surveillance camera in Global Coffee Shop, you and her met around the same period of time she was murdered."

"Murdered? What!?" she said in shock, knowing exactly who did it.

"I was hoping you can tell me what happened."

"I don't know, I really don't..." she said, frightened at this point as she tried to keep it together.

"So, what were you guys arguing about? looking at the camera, it looks like you two were arguing about something."

"Nothing really, just disagreements like friends have sometimes."

"But it looked pretty intense."

"It wasn't a big deal."

"So, what was it?"

"It was umm... just a little fight. It's personal."

"I need to know so I can try to rule you out."

"Rule me out from what? I didn't kill her!"

I didn't say that, but what a coincidence that she got murdered right after you two got into an argument about something you're clearly not telling me about."

"Did you also see that we left separately?"

"I did, but that's not enough. It could've been a setup."

"I didn't set her up, I swear." her heart raced rapidly.

"Look, you are going to have to give me something."

"I don't know what to give you, but I know I didn't kill her."

"Okay then, we will keep in touch."

"So, I'm free to go?" She said with fear in her tone.

"Yes, unless you have something to tell me before it's too late."

"I don't know what you want me to say."

"Your dad is a lawyer, right?"

"Yes?"

"Ok, good. I will keep in touch."

"What does my dad being a lawyer have to do with this?"

"Just in case you need him when I do find out what really hap-pened."

"So, you don't believe me?"

"You didn't tell me anything to believe."

"I don't have anything to say."

"Ok then, this really concludes our interview. I will be in touch. But here is my card just in case you decide to talk." She snatched his card and left.

She walked outside and felt relieved for not falling into the de-tective's trap. But she knew this was far from over with the way the detective spoke to her.

She was filled with rage as she drove straight to Allen's house with tears in her eyes. She could barely see straight with the tears com-ing down her eye. Davina was so scared and frustrated that the po-lice were closing in on them after Nita's death. She just knew that they had lost control on the situation, the moment Allen took matters into his hands. "What the fuck was he thinking?" she said with anger as she pulled up to his house. She parked on the drive-way and stormed to the door while wiping the tears off her face.

She got in front of the door and banged on it with rage. She did not stop until someone opened the door. This time it wasn't Allen, it was his friend Clay.

"Where is Allen?" She asked as she walked in, ready to snap.

I don't know why?" He said calmly knowing why she was here.

"Nita is dead... freaking dead!!" She said furiously.

"And?"

"And? Is that all you have to say?"

"What am I supposed to say? You said the girl is dead right?"

"Fucking unbelievable! So, you knew about this huh?"

"I don't know what you're talking about." He said with a slight bit of irritation in his tone, trying not to lose it with her.

"Why are you so loyal to him after everything he has done?" Davina said, stepping up to Clay.

"Why are you not loyal to him after all he has done for you?" he said, letting the demon in him come out, as he moved towards her while she backed away in fear. "You know I could've killed you a long time ago, but he just wouldn't let me." He said as he kept walking towards her until he backed her into a corner. He could see the fear in her face, and he was enjoying every moment of it. He never liked her, he saw her weakness the night of the accident, and he knew she would be trouble unless they got rid of her on time; Allen wouldn't let him. He looked her up and down then continued "I really don't know what he sees in you to want to save your life when it's not worth the risk. Stay out of his way if you know what's good for you." He said before stepping out of her way. "You can see your way out!" he concluded before walking away as Davina left in a hurry still in fear. He wanted to end her life the moment he had the chance, but he knew Allen would bring war upon him; he didn't want to lose the only human he really cared about other than the family he had left.

CHAPTER 26

Clayton was a heartless creature; he had been that way ever since after high school. His life wasn't that bad, considering the dysfunctional home that he came from. He loved his family, especially his father who became the remedy to his downfall; he wanted to be just like him, until tragedy hit, and he found himself in a dark hole he couldn't get himself out of.

Clayton was born to a well-known and respected father. His father was the best drug dealer on the whole block. People from other cities came to his block just to buy from him. He was the only supplier on that block unless someone came looking for trouble. His popularity from selling dope was the way he recruited enemies along with the feds whose mission was to bring him down. They sat back and waited for the day that they'd find something solid on him. Clayton's father Tony never handled anything by himself, so it was hard to catch him with anything solid. He had people handling his business and kept everything in the shadows as much as possible. Even though his business was low key, his love for 'women' wasn't. He believed his only curse in this world was his addiction to women. Money wouldn't keep Tony faithful to women. The girls didn't complain much, and he couldn't have it any other way; He loved his life and the big family he made with different mothers to his kids. Gloria was his main woman who stood behind him through the heartbreak, cheating, trouble and pain. She couldn't handle leaving him, so she stayed and dealt with it until one day, Tony brought a woman who was holding a baby in her arms to the house.

"Hey baby!" Tony said with excitement to Gloria as he walked in with a woman who was holding a baby in a blue blanket.

"Who is she and what is she doing here?" Gloria said with a serious face as her heart beat out of rhythm; she knew something was up.

"This is Tina, and the little boy she is holding is my son." Her heart skipped as the fear unraveled at the moment those words poured out of his mouth. She knew something was going on with him not being at home lately, she just didn't know why he was always gone. But she knew the story he was telling her about being absent was bullshit. She felt numb and broken. Her vulnerability felt the true pain and it hurt like pins and needles placed on the surface of her heart. She stood still and couldn't speak, but they stood there waiting for a response.

"What the fuck is she doing here?" She finally spoke after breaking her frustration. She asked herself why this was happening, while they've been actively trying to have another baby in hopes for a boy this time. Tony has nine children which were all girls, not including the little boy that they were holding in their living room. They had three kids together and six outside of their relationship. He had three before he met her and three more when he cheated on her.

"I was thinking she can stay here with us."

"Well, you thought wrong."

"I'm sorry for even coming here." Tina said as she tried walking away.

"No, you stay right here!" Tony said, then faced Gloria who was shaking out of control. "You want me to drive the mother of my son away with my son?"

"You know what? She can stay, I will leave." She said as she walked past them to enter her room.

"No wait!" Tony said, trying to pull her back.

"DON'T YOU PUT YOUR FUCKING HANDS ON ME…" she shouted. "How dare you Tony…after all these fucking years with you huh? How fucking dare you?" She was full of rage with tears falling down her chin; her life was shattered right before her eyes.

"I'm sorry!!" Tony pleaded.

 "You're always sorry, you sorry ass bastard." She said as she faced Tina, who was scared standing by Tony with the baby in her arms. "You can have it all: this house, this piece of shit of a man, EVERYTHING! Take it because I am done!!" She stormed away from them breathing out of control, as she went straight to the backyard to interrupt her two younger children playing with their friends. She didn't want to pull them away from their home and friends, but she was done with Tony's rollercoaster of hurt and pain.

"Girls come on let's go."

"But we are still playing." Pearl, one of her daughters said.

"I said come in here, let's go!!" she said as they grumbled inside. She went to her oldest daughter's room "hey sweetie, pack what you can; we are going to your grandmother's house."

"Why mom?" she asked, but she wasn't surprised that her parents were fighting again, she was used to their arguments.

"I will explain later, just do what I said and help your sisters pack too. We need to leave now!"

CHAPTER 27

Gloria moved out from the house she shared with her fiancée back to her mother's house with their three children. She was so hurt, to the point she could barely think straight. A life without Tony was a life she never imagined for herself. She couldn't hide her hurt from anybody; it was right on her sleeves. Each day became a struggle for her and their kids. They wanted to go home, but she wasn't ready; she would always tell them 'soon'. Amber the oldest knew something was wrong, when she saw a woman with a baby standing next to her father in their living room before they left. She asked her mother who the lady was, but she would always tell her she was nobody. She never really wanted to talk about it until her best friend Adrena came to visit her one day. to visit.

"So, you really just going to let that bitch take over your house and fiancée and do nothing?" Her best friend Adrena said to her. She had always been the friend who never sugarcoat anything with her no matter how fucked up she was feeling.

"What am I supposed to do?" she said with her heart heavy in pain.

"Fight back!!"

"I am not about to fight that little bitch over his fucking ass." She said furiously. "She can have the fucking house and him because I am done." Those words strike another pain into her heart as she kept trying to convince herself that it was over for good.

"Who said anything about fist fighting? Although it wouldn't be a bad idea to knock her ass out for being a homewrecker."

"Girl…every part of me wanted to, but my kids were somewhere in the house. And besides, she is not my problem, he did this."

"Fuck that, they both did this; she knew he was with you and she still did what she did anyway. And now he moved her in with that baby that may not even be his!" she said, rolling her eyes.

"I wanted to have a boy with him so bad, but God wasn't blessing me with one; he kept giving me girls." She said with emotions.

"You still have time to give that nigga a boy, you just have to find a way to get rid of the homewrecker whether Tony is the father or not."

"How? and besides, I think he is the father, and he will always be the first son of his." She said with her emotions running high as the tears came down.

"And??? Look, stop thinking too much and listen to me. If you want him back, you can't accomplish that by hiding here at your mama's house. You are going to have to get your ass up and move your ass back into that house. He is your fiancée, not hers."

"You're right!" she said with a cracked tone of voice as she wiped her tears. Her heart was beating fast with pain and confusion.

"I know I'm right! So, what are you going to do? Sit here and hope things get better or get your ass back into that house and make the bitch uncomfortable and hopefully, she will run off before you know it."

"I don't know…"

"Ok then, suite yourself. But before I go, just know the heart has a mind of its own. Listen to your heart." she grabbed her purse and left her in her thoughts. Gloria knew if she listens to her heart, she will be right back at that house with her kids; despite the mistress that is currently living in there.

Two weeks had gone by with her still debating on what to do. She couldn't come to a conclusion; she just knew in her heart she still loved him.

"I want to go home mom!" her daughter Amber said as she burst into her room where she was laying down, deep in thoughts.

"Why? you don't like it here?" her mom responded.

"I do. But I miss my friends, my house, my school and my dad."

"But we can also start a new life here with new friends, new school and you can always go see your dad anytime you want."

"Why can't we just go back home? I hate being here and sharing rooms."

"This is your new home for now until I figure things out."

"That's not fair; I don't want to be here. I don't even know why you left in the first place because you are not telling me anything." She said with frustration.

"I understand, but you just have to be patient with me to figure things out ok?"

"For how long? School is about to start, and I want to be back home before school starts."

"What if we check out the schools out here to see what it's like?"

"No thank you."

"But we may need to stay here for a little while. So, I suggest you get a little comfortable and stop being so close minded about everything." She said with a slight bit of irritation.

"Nobody asked you to leave daddy's house, you could've just left me there instead of dragging me along with your mess."

"You watch your mouth little girl and go to your room."

"WHAT ROOM?" she shouted with anger, then marched out before her mother could say anything else to her. She felt guilty for moving them out of their home without considering how it would make them feel; she was only thinking about her hurt for the moment.

The part that hurt the most was not the fact he cheated; it was the fact he got somebody else pregnant with a boy she had always dreamt of having with him. It crushed her even more when he decided to move her to the home they shared together with their kids.

CHAPTER 28

She was devastated and still could not believe this was all happening to her; she kept hoping this was all a nightmare that she would wake up from soon. She knew he had been cheating during their eight years of engagement, but also knew in her heart that nobody was important to him enough to take her position until now. She kept thinking about this woman coming and taking everything, she has ever built with him. "Fuck that!!!" She said as she got up from her bed, tired of torturing herself over going back. She then marched to the room where her children were doing homework for their new school. "Hey girls, are you guys ready to go back home for good?" She said with a smile on her face. But deep inside her heart was beating with fear; not knowing how it would be, going back home when the woman was still there.

"What home?" Amber the oldest one asked with confusion.

"Your home with your dad!" she said while still smiling.

"Really?" Amber said with excitement as she jumped up.

"Yes, honey really…"

"When?"

"Now!!!" she said with excitement. She was happy to see her children happy again; they haven't been in the best mood ever since she uprooted them from their home. She tried not to think about what they would be facing when they got back there; she just knew she wasn't moving them back out of the house again.

"Are you sure mom?"

"Of course, honey; we will leave when you girls are done packing."

"Ok!" Amber said with excitement as she ran to the closet, ready to start packing.

"But what about our homework? we don't have to do it anymore?" Her second daughter Reena said.

"Nope… toss it because you all are going back to your original school."

"Thank you, mom, you are the best!!!" the oldest daughter said with excitement, as she hugged her mother tight.

"You're welcome…" she said hugging her back. with her heart full of joy to see how excited her kids finally were.

"Aint no bitch about to run me off my goddamn house…" she said to herself as she walked back to her room and started to pack as well.

"What's going on? The kids sound so happy." Gloria's mother said as she walked into Gloria's room.

"I am taking them back home!"

"Home where?" she said confused, knowing why they left in the first place.

"Our home with their father."

"Didn't he move another woman in? unless she moved back out already?"

"I'm sure she is still there mother, but who cares? My kids want to go back home and that's what I am going to do."

"So, what are you going to do when you get there? Kick the woman out?"

"I don't know what's going to happen mother but aren't nobody about to put me out of my own house."

"You should think about this before you move back."

"I have mom. I feel like it was unfair that I moved my kids out of their home that they've known all their life, all because he made a bad decision."

"I know, he was wrong for that. But what if he wants her to stay there?"

"Then we will all be in the same household until I run her off."

"This does not sound like a good idea darling." she said with concern.

"It's ok mother, everything is going to be alright. Besides, you told me to fight for what I want and never give up."

"This situation is different; you will look desperate if you move back in."

"I don't care how it looks mom, all I know is I am not going to let that little girl and that son of hers run me off."

"I know honey but think about this before you make this move back."

"I already did. But don't worry, everything will be ok I promise."

"But don't you want to leave the kids here just in case things don't go how you want?"

"No mother, they are the reason I am moving back. They miss their home, their school, and their friends there. This woman won't be the reason my kids won't be happy."

"So, does that mean you are going to tell the kids the truth about who the woman is and the little boy?"

"Eventually, just one step at a time." She said, then came closer to her and placed both hands on her shoulder "Don't worry, everything will be alright I promise."

Her mother exhaled then said, "ok then, I am here whenever you need me, or if you need to come back."

"Thanks mom, we will be back to visit as usual."

 "Ok then, just be careful."

"I will," Gloria said with a smile then went back to packing.

Her and her kids were all packed up and ready to go back home. The kids threw out all the books for their new school and hugged their grandmother goodbye before running off to the car.

CHAPTER 29

Gloria pulled into the driveway of their home, as the kids jumped out of the car and ran towards the door. They banged on the door impatiently, ready to see their father again. "Stop banging on the door and come get your bags."

Tina the new woman opened the door before they could turn around to get their bags. She was shocked to see them come back.

"Hello!" she said to the kids who turned around to her.

"Hi." The oldest said flatly.

"Girls come get your bags." Gloria said as she looked at the woman who almost stole her entire life up and down, with disgust in her face.

"Ok mom!" the oldest child Amber said as they came back to grab their bags.

"Do you guys need any help with carrying anything in?" she said nervously; She knew with them moving back in, won't be good for her.

"Of course not, we got it." Gloria said with an attitude. They went in with the bags they could carry, leaving Tina outside who was still in shock to see them there. Everyone's room still looked the same, except for Gloria and Tony's, which was now filled with Tina and the new baby's stuff. Gloria's anger exploded after seeing the changes they made in her room.

"I'm sorry I didn't think you were coming back." Tina said seeing Gloria's facial expression when she saw the way the room looked.

"So that gave you the right to move in my room?"

"Look, I am sorry about this whole situation; I didn't mean to interrupt your life like this."

"But you did, even when you knew he had a whole family at home." She said without holding back.

"All I can do is apologize."

"And what is that going to change huh?"

"I don't know, I just hope you forgive me eventually."

"So, you want me to forgive you, but yet you moved into my room with my man?"

"You left!!" She said with irritation. Gloria didn't care, she kept going without hesitation.

"That still doesn't give you the right to move in still."

"What was I supposed to do?"

"Decline moving in here when you saw what it was."

"I just wanted my child to have her father around."

"Look, I don't have time to stand here and go back and forth with you. You can stay here all you want, but it won't be in this room and be prepared for a life in hell under this roof." She said while walking away to get more stuff from the car.

"Why are you blaming me for this huh? I am not the one who cheated on you and brought me here."

"Bitch you still have a lot of balls to be talking after what you did. You are lucky my kids are under this roof right now. If not, your lips would've been too swollen to be talking back. Get your shit out now!" she said standing firmly in Tina's face, as she boils in anger.

"You know what? I don't need this; I will get my stuff and leave this house." Tina said, stepping out of her face.

"Even better." Gloria replied.

"I am not the one you should be mad at; he is the one that cheated on you. But yet you are mad at me?"

"You don't worry about what i am going to do to him, I will deal with him on my own. As for you, you knew what it was thot."

"Oh, now I'm a thot?" she said laughing through the anger she was feeling.

"What did you think you were, after sleeping with a man who was engaged with three Children."

"Um you have been engaged now for how long?" she mocked.

"you don't worry about it; just know he has been off the market for God knows how long."

"He clearly doesn't know that if he is still sleeping around."

"You just want to get fucked up bad, don't you?" Gloria said with a chuckle.

"I'm not doing this shit in front of my child; I will come get my things later." She walked towards the bed to get her son.

"They will be packed and ready for you when you come get them." She didn't respond back, she just let the tear come down her eyes as she packed a few of their things.

CHAPTER 30

Shortly after, Tony walked into the room to see Gloria arranging her stuff back to where it was before she left. Tina and her son's stuff were packed up and placed in the hallway.

"Hey..." he said confused.

"Hey." She responded back knowing why he looked confused.

"you're back."

"I sure am!"

"Where is Tina?"

"How about you call her and ask. I'm sure you have her number on the speed dial." He took out his phone and stepped out and called her.

"Hey where are you?"

"Don't worry about it, just know we are fine."

"What happened?"

"What do you think? You moved me in a house that you and your fiancée shared, and you thought she was just going to accept that?"

"But she left..."

"And now she is back."

"look I'm sorry, it was not my intention to create this mess."

"but you did."

"I'm sorry, I will fix it. I just wanted to wake up with my son every day."

"So, you thought she was going to be just cool with me staying there without a problem? I told you from the beginning it will be a problem, but you said it will be cool."

"The plan was to have you in your own room with my son, but she ended up leaving. I still want you here so I can see my son every day."

"I am not doing that Tony, she is already fucking pissed that you had a baby outside your relationship, and now you want me there? I knew this was a bad idea from the beginning. From now on, I am going to continue to stay with my roommate until you can get us a place of our own. This is your mess, fix it."

"I will." He said rubbing his bald head with a lot on his mind "I will be there later to see my son."

"Don't bother to come today, we will see you tomorrow."

"See... that's why I want you here. I don't need you or anybody telling me when I'm supposed to see my fucking son."

"you put yourself in this situation, deal with it."

"I know I did." He signed.

"I felt bad from the beginning for interrupting your life with your kids and fiancée, but you told me it wasn't like that, which was why I was still fucking with you. Now we have a baby together and we just must find a way to be a good coparent, nothing else."

"So, you're saying you're going to be seeing other people too?"

"Eventually. What? You want me to be single for the rest of my life?"

"I can be your man too."

"Nigga you sound stupid and selfish as hell. I am not doing that shit with you. I messed up by agreeing to move in with you so my son can be around his family, and because you told me she would be cool with it. I should've moved my ass out the moment she packed her shit and her kids and left. That was my bad, I won't be that naïve and stupid again."

"I'm sorry for putting you in that situation, I thought it would have worked; I just wanted to be close to my son."

"You thought wrong. Do you know how humiliating it was when she kicked me out of the room with my son laying there? It was very embarrassing. And now it is going to be harder for her and the kids to warm up to us."

"Don't worry about that, I will fix it."

"You better."

"Just trust me that everything is going to be ok"

"I don't know that, but I do hope that you can get things back to normal whereas my son can get to know his siblings."

"I will, I promise." He said before she hung up.

He went back in the room to see Gloria wiping things down. She packed more of Tina's stuff in the trash bag that was by the closet and had already changed the sheets and blankets on their bed.

"I am sorry for not checking in with you first before moving them in, but you know how much I wanted a boy"

"yeah! and I wanted one too. So, you should know how it made me feel when you moved the side chick in with a baby boy in her hand."

"I'm sorry I wasn't thinking, I just wanted my children in the same household."

"That would never happen if they aren't mine. What about the other baby mothers huh? So, you're going to move them in too since you want all your goddamn kids together huh?"

"I'm sorry!"

"I don't know what makes you think this shit was ok. You moving them in hurts more than you getting her pregnant."

"I know, but that's my only boy. I just wanted him closer to me."

"At the expense of me being unhappy?"

"I never wanted you to be unhappy."

"Then why the fuck will you bring your side chick to my mother-fucking house?"

"I don't know, I am sorry, I just thought we can all get along for the sake of the kids."

"You moving her in would be the opposite of that. You've been bold as fuck lately like I wasn't going to do shit."

"That's not true!"

"Then what made you think it was ok to move her in with her son?"

"That's my son too."

"You made that clear already. Look, because I let you slide with your past infidelity don't mean I'm ok with it."

"I know, I'm sorry."

"I'm sure you are with your sorry ass." She said before walking away from him, to continue her cleaning.

"It won't happen again..."

"Oh, I know it won't, because it won't be pretty next time. It's already bad enough you got her pregnant with a boy that I've always wanted. I wanted to give you a son so bad, but it just wasn't happening. I wasn't giving up in trying until you pulled this shit."

"I'm sorry, I fucked up bad and I will clean it up."

"You can't clean this up; she already had your baby. All we can do now is deal with it and hope things don't get out of control."

"It won't."

"Oh, you can tell the future now?"

"No, but I will do my best to keep it in control."

"We will see." she said as she continued to wipe down while Tony went to see their children's bedroom; they were getting situated and settled in their own individual rooms.

CHAPTER 31

Eventually Tina and Gloria started to get along for the sake of the children. Clayton Tina's son would come whenever he pleased. Tony was still in and out of the house, heavy in the drug game. He was very successful, and people knew better than to sell products on Tony's block unless it belonged to him. He only showed a soft side when it came to his family and close friends; they knew he wasn't the one to cross or piss off.

 "I will be back, I'm just stepping out with Andrew real quick." Tony said to Gloria one day.

"Clayton is on his way here; he just got back from his field trip and have some good news to tell you."

"I'm sure whatever it is can wait, I'm just stepping out briefly. I will be back before you even know it."

"Ok then, just hurry up because I want to hear what he has to say. I think he got accepted to the school he has always wanted to go to, because he sounded so excited on the phone."

"That's good news. But this is important, I will be back."

"Can't Andrew handle it on his own like he always does?"

"I know, but he wants me there; it must be serious. Some fuckers may be playing with my money, so let me go see about it. I will be back soon I promise." He said as he placed a kiss on her lips.

"But that can wait, he is almost here."

"Clay can wait. Tell him daddy will be back soon."

"Ok then."

He drove to Andrew's and picked him up.

"What's going on?" Tony asked while Andrew got in the car.

"Yo Mike got robbed"

"whatcu you mean he got robbed?" he said with a big frown on his face.

"Yeah man, he was delivering a package to somebody at the south side and he got ambushed and robbed."

"Who is somebody? I need names man!"

"I don't know, we are about to find out."

"How much worth of coke was he delivering?"

"20 stacks!"

"Twenty thousand? Hell no I need names asap. Motherfuckers knew not to try me like that."

"Yeah, I don't know, that shit was crazy."

"I hope Mike aren't fucking with me, I don't play with my money period."

"He is not, he knows better."

"Aright then, let's pull up and see wassup."

CHAPTER 32

Tony and Drew came to the lot where they stored all their goods and supplies, then drove to the back. They got out of the car ready to confront Mike, who was standing firm next to Ron, as they waited for this moment that was about to come.

"Yo what the hell happened?" Tony said then suddenly, Drew pointed a gun at Tony's head from behind. Tony tried to quickly reach for his gun as Drew shot him in his hand, causing him to lose control of his gun as it fell to the ground.

"What the fuck man? What the fuck are you doing?" Tony said, holding on to his bloody hand in pain.

"We are tired of working for you that's all, and the only way out is for you to be 6 feet under." Drew said calmly.

"So, you're going to take my life just to make that happen?" He said in panic and hurt that his best man had turned on him.

"That's the only way!" Drew said, still in a calm voice. He knew this had to happen, there was no going back now.

"That's not the only way man; you can have it if you want. You just can't take me away from my family like that man."

"you must think we are some boo boo the fool to think you are just going to let us take over while you back off?"

"I will man, if that's what ya want." He said in fear, knowing that there was no possibility he was walking out of this lot alive.

"Na, what we want is for you to be completely out of the way." He said then shot him twice in the head as they watched his body drop to the ground. They all felt peace and relieved that he was no longer in their way of taking over.

"Make sure every single place is clean. I don't want them tracing anything back to us; clean up the gun and everything in here just in case his filthy blood got on anything. We can't go down for this, he deserved to die." Andrew said, feeling the relief that he was no longer in Tony's shadow; he felt in charge.
"What about the body?" Mike asked.
"Our enemies wanted him dead, that's where they will find his body."

"Are you trying to pin this shit on them? they will kill us all if they find out."
"Exactly!! that's why they will never find out." Drew said.

 "But the important thing right now is, how are we going to run this shit now that Tony is gone." Mike asked.

"I will let you know when y'all take care of this body; get to work so we can get back to work."

"Nigga why are you talking like you're about to be in charge and shit?"

"Who else will? Somebody got to run this shit."
"I ain't never liked your ass, so what makes you think I want to work for you?" Mike said
"Well I'm next in line, that's just how it's going to be."
" I still ain't working for you nigga. The plan was we run this shit together, NO leader!"
"Look around my nigga; this is a whole lot of shit. I know how to make this whole shit go smooth and we will still get our cut evenly."

"I don't trust that shit, I'm out." While he was walking out, Drew shot him in the back and kept shooting as he got closer.

"What the fuck!!!!" Ron said in disbelief as his eyes got wider, he couldn't believe what just happened.

"He can't be trusted by the way he was talking."

"So that means he got to die?"

"Yes, he may rat us out!"

"You are getting out of control my nigga, you just killed two of our people. What the fuck man…" He said, in extreme rage. He was pissed and hurt at the same time.

"You want to go to jail?"

"No nigga, but two bodies from our side may land us right in there."

"We got to take them away towards our enemies at the North side. They won't know this was from us I promise."

"What if someone catches us pulling out two dead bodies out of the fucking car huh?"

"You're tripping hard right now, it's not a good look."

"What? Are you going to kill me too huh nigga?" he said as he got in his face with anger.

"Of course, not my nigga, I will never do that shit."

"But you just did it to two of them. You are fucking tripping man!"

"You knew Tony was dying today, why are you acting like you were blindsided or something."

"I didn't know Mike was."

"He can't be trusted!"

"Because he said he didn't want no leader? That we were supposed to do this shit together? Because that's the same shit I want and that's what Tony died for."

"I know, but somebody got to run this shit though."

"Why? When we can do this shit together and make the decisions together."

"Ok, if that's how you want it, so be it."

"Yes, that's exactly how I wanted it. And you killed Mike for nothing!"

"He would've stitched…"

"No, he wouldn't have. He was my motherfucking partner in all of this shit man, and you took his life like he meant nothing!" he said still with anger.

"I'm sorry, I thought he was going to snitch."

"Well, you thought motherfucking wrong my nigga. You are just fucking out of control."

"I'm sorry man, I don't know what else to say, I can't bring the nigga back, I'm fucking sorry."

"Don't be sorry, get it together so nobody else will have to die…" he said as he walked away.

"Where are you going?"

"Home my nigga, where else?" he said with anger and frustration. He was still brewing inside.

"Who is going to help me get rid of these bodies?"

"I ain't doing shit, I've had enough from today. You killed them, now you clean this shit up by your goddamn self."

"I'm sorry, I aint mean to do that."

"Whatever man, I'm out." he said as he started to walk away, then turned around "Oh and be ready to tell their family and kids that their fucking father is dead and never EVER coming home to them, because of your unstable ass."

"Man… why are you acting like you didn't know tony was dying today."

"Yeah, but I didn't know Mike was too though."

"I said I'm sorry."

"Yeah, like that shit will bring him back."

"I don't know what else to say."

"Just clean this shit up, and we will figure things out later when shit dies down."

"What about work."

"You want to talk about work at a time like this?"

"You're right" Drew said, as Ron walked away in pain from the tragic death of his close friend. He went home feeling torn. He didn't know if he should turn Drew in or not. He knew if he decided to turn him in, Drew will drag him down for the murder as well. He was lost and confused on what he should do.

CHAPTER 33

Few days later, they found the bodies exactly where Drew planned it. The families of the victims were crushed and broken when they found out. They just couldn't believe what was happening. Gloria didn't take it well. A piece of her died the moment she found out Tony was dead. She was so hurt that she didn't know what to do. She kept fighting the thought of her becoming both the man and woman of the house without Tony. He was the love of her life and now he was gone forever.

 days later, Drew went to Tony's house to give his condolences. Gloria didn't trust Drew. She still believed he knew something more; and he isn't telling anyone about it.

"So, what really happened? You were the last person with him, right?" Gloria questioned. She kept fidgeting with anger and impatience, knowing Drew has something up his sleeve. She had always warned Tony to be careful with him because she simply didn't trust him.

"I don't know after he dropped me off."

"I thought ya went to go check on Mike about him being robbed..." She said, raising an eyebrow.

"He did get robbed, and he dropped me off afterwards."

So, you mean to tell me that my fiancée and the person ya went to go see about is dead? How Drew, talk to me because nothing is making sense."

"I told you what happened, I don't know what else to tell you." He said, getting frustrated trying to get through to her.

"I don't believe you for shit… I told his ass not to trust you." She said standing in his face with anger and rage.

"I swear I have nothing to do with it, but I will find his killer I promise."

"So, you're turning yourself in then? Because I know you are the killer!"

"I didn't do it, I swear."

"Why are you even here? You don't think we've suffered enough? You took away my fiancé, their father and then you come here to say what? That you didn't do it? You are bold as fuck and disrespectful for even showing your face here!"

"I am so sorry; I wish you could just know that I didn't do it."

"So, you want me to believe a lie? And you being sorry will never bring him back! But justice will bring some kind of peace to this family; and I won't give up until justice is served." She said as he walked away feeling uneasy and heavy hearted for being the cause of their pain. "You've destroyed us all, and I hope you never find peace for the rest of your life; even when you decide to do the right thing and turn yourself in." He walked out without saying another word. He knew there was nothing else to do to solve this; but only to tell the truth which in reality, that was the furthest thing from his mind. He wasn't going to let his family go through the same pain that Mike and Tony's family was going through.

As for Ron, he couldn't let the guilt of not speaking up continue to eat him alive. He spoke up and threw himself under the bus before Drew did it for him. Drew was sentenced to life without the possibility of parole and Ron was sentenced to 15 years. Even with justice being served, Tony's family was never the same. Clay went downhill and never came back up. The day his father was killed, was the day he was going to tell him that he was accepted to the college he always wanted to go and play ball at. He didn't go to school after that, he just kept going down the wrong path to land himself in jail every time. During one of his stay in jail, he met

Allen who took him under his wings and taught him how to cover his tracks without consequences.

CHAPTER 34

(Back to present)

"What the fuck do I do?" Davina said in tears while driving home from Allen's house. The way Clayton spoke to her had her scared for her life. She knew going to the police would only set him off even more.

She drove home in tears not knowing what to do. She got home and went straight to her room and curled up in her bed with a heavy heart. Everything was falling apart and there was nothing she could do to stop it.

"How the fuck did this happen?" she said with frustration while crying in her bed.

"Davina!!" her dad screamed from downstairs as he made his way speedily towards her room. She jumped up from her bed, knowing he knew something by the way he was screaming and running upstairs "Davina!!" he said again when he got up in her room.

"Yes daddy" she said with a shaky voice.

"What the fuck is going on?" her dad Darnel screamed, he feared knowing that she had gotten herself into something bad.

"I don't know what you're talking about daddy..." she lied.

"Lie to me one more time and I will hand you right to the fucking police."

"I don't know daddy…" she said, as she burst out in tears.

"How are you in the middle of these two major incidents huh? Explain that to me, because I am beginning to think you know more than you have been telling me."

"Dad, I don't know." She said, still defending herself.

Her dad took a deep breath then sat on her computer chair. "I can't protect you if you don't tell me anything. They will come for you and when they do, I wouldn't know how to save you because I don't know anything." He said calmly. She didn't say anything but was still in tears. He got up to walk away.

"Daddy wait…" she said as he stopped and turned around to face her. "I didn't do it I swear."

"Then who?" he said with frustration.

She was silent again "ok then, you are on your own." He said as he was about to walk away from again.

"Allen!"

"Your so-called boyfriend?"

"Yes him"

"What about him?"

"He…" she got quiet again, didn't know where to start. The only thing that was consistent at this point with her was the tears that were coming down her cheeks.

"Damit Davina, tell me something!"

"I don't know!"

"You don't know what?"

"I think Allen killed Nita."

"You think or you know!" He said still frustrated that she was not getting straight to the point.

"He did!"

"Why would he want to kill Nita?"

"Because she was giving Sia ideals about that night."

"What night?"

"The night of the accident."

"What about that night? What did you guys do?"

"I didn't do anything!!"

"Ok… Davina you will need to break this down for me, because I'm really confused right now."

"Ok. But daddy, I swear I didn't have anything to do with it."

"You need to explain this shit to me because it seems like you're in the middle of this whole fucking mess!!" Darnel said with anger, not caring about the way he was talking to her. He was more afraid of losing another child.

"I didn't do anything I swear."

"Then what the fuck happened?"

"What's going on?" Davina's mother came up after hearing the noise upstairs

"Your daughter is about to really tell me what happened on the night of that accident that landed her friend Sia to prison."

"She did already!"

"No, she told us what she wanted us to know, not the whole truth."

"Davina, what is your dad talking about?" Rebecca said, facing her daughter.

"I need you to leave so I can finish talking to our daughter." Darnel said with his face full of concern.

"No, I'm staying to hear what she has to say!" she said with panic.

"So, who was driving that night?" Darnel asked.

"Allen."

"Allen?" Her mother said in shock.

"Yes!" she said with her head down as she let out more tears.

"So how did Sia get in front of the seat?" her dad asked with a straight face.

"Allen placed her there."

 "So you knew about this all along?"

"How will she know when she was asleep too?" Rebecca interrupted, coming to Davina's defense.

"Can you let her talk to me? That's the only way I can save her." He said with an irritable voice.

"Yes." Davina answered.

"Yes what?" Darnel said.

"Allen was the one driving. He also came up with the idea to place Sia in the driver's seat, which made it seem like she was the one driving." She said with more tears rolling down her cheeks.

 "Oh my God no!! Davina, what have you done?" she said with fear in her voice.

 "Ok Davina, I need you to take a deep breath and tell me everything that happened that night, and how it led to Nita being killed."

"That night, Nita kind of knew Sia wasn't driving because I told her she was too drunk to drive. She has been visiting Sia and telling her to investigate more by looking at cameras, to see who was really driving that night. I told Allen and..." She paused as tears came down her eyes, then she continued "and he told me to meet her somewhere, that he will take care of it afterwards if I couldn't convince her to keep quiet."

"And then what?" her father pressed even more.

"I think he followed her home and killed her, since I couldn't convince her to keep quiet."

"How would you know he followed her home?"

"Because I called him afterwards to let him know I couldn't convince her to keep quiet. Then he said he would take care of it. I tried to ask what his plan was, but he wouldn't tell me. He said don't worry about it, then he hung up."

"So he followed her from the coffee shop?"

"Yes."

Rebecca sat on Davina's bed, listening to what her daughter was saying and trying to take it all in. She was afraid it wasn't looking good for her.

"So that means he was already there waiting while you girls were inside?"

"Yes."

"Did you see him while he was there?"

"No."

"How would you know he was the one that followed her and killed her then?"

"Because he was the only one that wanted her out of the picture, so she won't snitch or lead Sia to the truth. He was also the only one that knew where we were."

"Have you spoken to him since the incident?"

"No."

"Ok good, don't speak to him until you hear back from me on what the next steps will be. I will be back."

"Ok daddy…" she said, wiping off her tears with a little relief from finally getting the truth off her chest.

"And also, when the police call you in for questioning, tell them what happened. If they ask you why you're just now coming forward about it, tell them you were afraid of him and what he might've done to you if you didn't follow his rules."

"But he didn't really threaten me."

"Do what I say, and you will walk away with either a few months or even a few years in jail."

"Jail?" Rebecca said with panic.

"Yes, do you think this is a joke?" Darnel said to Rebecca "an innocent girl has been in jail for this mess, while the other is dead all because your child was protecting a murderer." He paused then faced Davina "Nita would still be alive if you just said something from the beginning." Davina burst out in tears again, knowing her dad was right. He walked out of Davina's room as Rebecca followed behind him, leaving Davina who was still crying behind in the room.

"There has got to be something you can do!" Rebecca said

"Like what?"

"I don't know, you are the lawyer. Do something!"

"I am. We are going to paint Allen as the mastermind in this case and Davina was used by him."

"Were there more people behind this?" Rebecca asked.

"I don't know, go ask your daughter. But I will let you know if I find anything else." He said before he walked out of the house.

CHAPTER 35

Rebecca walked into Davina's room, who was curled up in her bed crying. She sat by the edge of the bed next to her daughter with her heart racing in fear. She knew however this end, it won't be good for her.

"Davina!" she sighed then continued "I need you to get it together and talk to me."

"Ok!" she said while trying to pull herself up. She was weak and tired from crying, but overall, she was mostly afraid of what her life was about to become once everything came out.

"Let's start from the beginning, who was all in the car when that accident happened?"

She wiped the tears from her face before answering her mother's question. "Me, Sia, Allen and Clayton."

"Who is Clayton?" she asked

"Allen's friend."

"Does he have any role in any of this?"

"He helped him with everything he did."

"That's not specific enough. What did he do pertain to these crimes Davina?" She said with irritation, as her heart beats fast for her daughter's fate.

"He was there when Allen had the accident; he went with the plans and he has also been covering for him too in everything he did, including Nita's death."

"How would you know that was you there when Nita was killed

too?" she said in panic.

"No… I knew because I just came from their house and when I told him what happened, he said 'and?'

"Where was Allen?"

"He wasn't there."

"Ok then, I'm about to go call your father to let him know about this too." She said with a heavy heart, not knowing how her daughter got herself into such a mess. She was falling apart on the inside; she tried her best to keep it together.

She left Davina's room to go get her phone and tell Darnel what Davina just told her.

"How the hell did she get herself in such a mess under our nose?"

"I don't know Darnel; all I know is I am not losing the only child I have left; do all you can to save our baby." She said, still trying her hardest not to break down.

"I will do all I can, but I need you two to stay home today and don't go anywhere until I return."

"Ok."

"And don't open the door for anybody, I have a key; I can let myself in."

"You think he may come after her?"

"I don't know, but he is a serial killer; I rather be safe than sorry at this point, especially when they know she may be talking."

"You don't know that."

"Are you willing to take a chance with a serial killer?" she got quiet. "I didn't think so. I will be there as soon as I can."

"Ok." She hung up and stayed in her room and cried. She was feeling everything a mother who was desperate to save her child was feeling.

CHAPTER 36

Davina drifted off after crying for hours as the rain hit the rooftop of her bedroom. She had a dream Sia walked out of jail to seek revenge "So you were just going to stand there and let him ruin my life huh?" she said with anger.

"No of course not, I was trying to find a way out for you."

"There is no way out for me, and there is no way out for you either." She rushed to grab Davina as she woke up rapidly from her nightmare. She was breathing heavily with panic. She laid back down trying to sleep away this unusual feeling; sleep wouldn't come, and the rain didn't stop falling. She was afraid now that everything was out.

She went downstairs since she couldn't fall asleep to get something to drink. She opened her fridge to grab a bottle of water. When she closed it, Clayton was standing by the side of the fridge. "Hello snitch!" he said as she gasped in fear hoping this was part of her nightmare. *'How did he get in my house'* she thought to herself frantically while swiftly backing away from him at a high speed. As she turned around to run, Allen was standing behind to stop her at her track; she could see the anger he was feeling in his eyes. "Allen, what are you doing here?" she said, trying to control her fear.

"So, you don't know why I'm here huh?"

"No!" she responded, as he slapped her in the face causing her to lose control and fell backwards to the ground. "You know I hate liars, right?" he said calmly, as he slowly came down towards her. "Allen, I didn't say anything, I swear!" she said while still on the ground; her hands were in her face as she choked out of control.

"How would anyone have a clue as to what happened to that bitch then?" he said with a frown face; he felt betrayed.

"I don't know…" she said as he slapped her again "I swear to God I will kill you right here along with anyone in this fucking house, if you lie to me again." He raised his voice in rage this time.

"Ok…ok…they knew I was the last person to see her before she died."

"How?"

"I met her at the coffee shop, remember?"

"And?"

"And…everyone likes coffee."

"Don't sass me bitch. How did they fucking know?"

"People talk Allen, they've been talking."

"No, your friend Nita was talking, which was why I eliminated her ass."

"Bad idea; now they're wondering why she is dead after she visited Sia, and then I saw her right after at the coffee shop."

"So why is my fucking face on the news as a suspect?"

"I don't know!" he grabbed her head and slammed it to the concrete ground in the kitchen floor with anger. "My dad!!" she said crying out loud with pain.

"Davina?" her mother called out to her after hearing noises downstairs.

Allen looked up at Clayton, then said "take care of her!" he ordered as Clay walked past them with a smile on his face.

"No, no… mommy go back…" Davina screamed.

"Shut up!" he mushed her face down as she kicked him in his nuts.

"ahhhh you bitch!!"

"Mom run...call the police!" Davina yelled. Her mother looked confused as she was coming downstairs. She saw a man quickly approaching her and she knew it had to be one of them. She turned back as quickly as she could, as Clayton took his first shot at her. The noise from the bullet made a loud ringing noise throughout the house. She dodged the bullet that was meant for her head. Davina made an attempt to run out of the house, but Clay spotted her and got back down just in time. He quickly slammed the door shut, allowing the door to forcedly hit Davina in the face.

 "Oooo... I've been waiting for this!" he said with his gun in hand, ready to end her life.

"Leave her for me and go take care of her upstairs." Allen said while coming towards them. His anger was out of control at this point.

"I got this one!" Clayton said with his eyes fixed on Davina.

"No you don't, now move!" he pushed Clayton out of Davina's face.

"Man!! ok, he said as he rushed back upstairs to hear her mother saying "hurry, my daughter is in danger" then additional words followed "I can't be on the phone I have to go!"

"Open this door!!" he said while banging on the door, in an attempt to find his way in. "Yo she called the police!" he also shouted out to Allen.

"You see what the fuck you've done huh?" he said as he threw her to the floor, then pulled out a gun.

"I am so sorry! I didn't think it would get this far."

"What the fuck do you mean?" Allen said, as Clay banged on the door upstairs trying to break his way in.

"I was just talking to my dad." she said, as he came closer and grabbed her by the hair.

"Right, your dad who is a freaking lawyer. How stupid can you fucking be huh?" he said pointing the gun to her face.

"I'm sorry..."

"You know what, you're a sorry ass bitch. Now let's go." He said, pulling her up.

"No... please, where?" she said, as he slapped her in the face with the gun he was holding.

"Don't fucking question me!" she fell to the ground, but quickly got back on her feet and ran back towards the kitchen. Allen shot at her and hit her shoulder, she screamed and kept running into the basement and locked it shut.

While upstairs, Clayton broke down the door and dragged her mother out by the hair. She tried to fight back with the hair iron she could find to defend herself; she lost as he dragged her downstairs.

When they got downstairs, Allen grabbed Davina's mother by the neck with a gun pointed to her head. He walked towards the basement and said "if you want your mother alive, come out wherever you are. I don't have time for this fucking game Davina." He said, still brewing in anger.

"Don't come out!" her mother shouted.

"SHUT UP!!" He screamed at her with rage as he held her neck tighter.

"Aaaahhh" Rebecca screamed.

"I can go down there and get her." Clayton requested with irritation that they are both still alive.

"You have my blessing. And hurry, didn't she call the fucking police?"

"Yup and don't worry, this won't be long!" he said with a grin on his face, as he moved quickly to the basement.

"No please don't, just take me instead." Rebecca pleaded; they ignored her as Clayton walked down to the basement in the dark. He quickly found the light switch and switched it on.

Davina was not in sight, but he saw the traces of blood. He followed quickly with a smile on his face. "You might as well come out, I can find you easy with your fucking bloody stains."

"Ok… ok… I will come with you, just leave my mother out of it." She said as she came out with her hands up like she was about to surrender.

"You are in no position to make demands" he said pinning her against the wall by her neck. "I don't know what he saw in you, but I'm happy he is back to his fucking senses" he said in disgust.

"Yo you got her?" Allen said loudly to Clayton, who was still down there with Davina. He was running out of patience knowing the police would be here any moment from now.

"Of course!" he said still pinning her to the wall.

"Ok, bring her ass and let's go!!" Allen furiously yelled before Clayton let go of her neck; she was trying to catch her breath while he dragged her upstairs. "Davina!! Her mother screamed in fear as she tried to run to her to help. Allen viciously pulled her back "Let's go!"

"No…stop! she is bleeding, I have to help her right now!" they ignored her request as they started to make their way out of the house. The police were already surrounding the house. They saw the car and two police officers slowly coming toward the house, while they pulled back away from the door.

"They are here!" Allen said in disappointment.

"Oh, shit what do we do? We have to get out of here?" Clayton said almost in a panic.

"It won't be that easy, come on!" he tried to pull Rebecca who struggled and screamed "help!!" he hit the gun across her head, and she passed out in his hand.

"Noooo you bastard!!" Davina tried to struggle but she was too weak. They quickly pulled them both through the back door.

"Freeze!!" four officers pointed at them as they pointed the gun to Davina and her mother's head. "they will be dead if you make a move!" Allen said as they quickly moved back in and got everywhere secured and locked, while the officers stayed outside and kept the place surrounded.

"What are we going to do?"

"I don't know"

Man, I can't go back to jail, what the fuck man!!"

"Shut the fuck up!! Let me fucking think."

"Think? We are fucking surrounded…" Clayton said as Allen pointed the gun at him.

"Man, I will kill you right the fuck now if you don't shut the fuck up." Allen said, then moved the gun from his face as he paced back and forth.

"Fuck!! this stupid bitch!!!" he said pointing to Rebecca who called the police. He went to Davina and pointed the gun to her face.

"Where's your phone?" Davina did not say anything, she was so weak from losing a lot of blood. "look, don't fucking play with me right now."

"Upstairs in my room "she said weakly. Allen ran upstairs to retrieve her phone.

"Here, put the password and call your father." He gave her the phone as she did as instructed, though she was starting to faint from losing a lot of blood.

"Dad!"

"Davina!! You ok?"

"No…" she said while in tears.

"Ok baby, I'm on my way." He said in tears also, knowing what was already going on. Allen grabbed the phone from her.

"It's good that you are on your way, but your daughter is over here very close to her grave. So, I suggest you send those idiotic officers back before your daughter and her mother dies."

"No please! you don't want to do that, think about it; you have a lot to lose."

"Like what?"

"Please anything you want me to do, I will do it."

"Now we are talking. Like I said, tell them to go or your family will die here."

"Please just let them go and we will talk."

"Ha, that was a good one. You or those officers outside don't give a fuck about me. So either you do what I say, or they die, what is it not to get?"

"Please I'm almost there, I will see what I can do when I get there."

"Oh, you think I'm playing huh?" he said as he took the phone off his ear, then took a picture while he was still on the phone pleading for their lives. He sent the picture to him of Davina laying there bloody and weak.

"No… no…you can't do this!" he said in tears, afraid that she may not make it if he keeps her longer.

"Well time is ticking for her."

"You don't want to do this please, let them go!"

"Then you need to get them out of my way if you want these two to see the next sunrise."

"Ok, let me talk to them now."

"You have five minutes to get them the fuck out of here."

"Ok" he said as he got off the phone and sped through the community. He jumped out of the car as the neighbors watched.

"I need everyone to go. That's the only way he will let my daughter and her mother live."

"We can't let them go; the house is surrounded." The detective in charge said.

"Well un-surround the house and go. My child's life is at risk and I am not letting her die." He said in panic.

"We won't let that happen. We just have to find a way in."

"There is no way that they won't see coming, just let them go!" he demanded.

"Sorry we can't do that."

"There has got to be another way to get them, but for now we don't have time. My daughter is bleeding to death."

"What if they don't release them?"

"Then you shoot them to the ground. You do whatever the fuck you need, to get my daughter and her mother back safe. So for now, pull them back." The senior commissioner thought about it, then called everyone back through the walkie talkie. They all reported to the front. "We will have to pull back, that's the only way he will let them go."

"We are just going to let them go?" one of the officers said.

"Of course not. Let's get the victim into our custody first, then we will do whatever it takes to get them."

"Copy."

"So for now, everyone drive off to a visible corner where you can't be seen. We will have to keep a close watch on them from a close distance, then we will be back to action right when they release them. It may have to be a race after they release them, just be ready for anything. Copy?"

"Copy." Another officer said as they all got in their car and left. They drove off to a place close by where they can't be seen, but visible enough to see who is coming in and out of the neighborhood. Davina's father called her phone and Allen picked up. "They are gone now, let them go." Darnel said as Allen hung up without saying a word. Shortly after, he came out with a gun in one hand and Davina who was not cautious in the other hand. Meanwhile Clayton was also holding a gun in one hand and Elizabeth who was just waking up in the other hand. "Darnel…" she said as she opened her eyes to see Darnel standing in front of the driveway anxiously. She then looked over to Davina "NO NO NO NO WHAT DID YOU DO?" she said, as she struggled her way out of Clayton's hand. Darnel stood aside impatiently, not wanting to trigger them to do anything other than letting them go.

"Let me go!!!" Rebecca said weakly with tears coming down her chin.

"Not until we get in the car. Now come on." Allen said to Clayton as they moved quickly towards the car. They looked around for anybody that could potentially ruin their plans of escaping. Darnel stayed out of their way, but behind them. They rushed to the car as Allen dropped Davina, while Clayton let Elizabeth go. Elizabeth and Darnel ran to Davina, as Clay and Allen ran to their car and drove off in full speed.

CHAPTER 37

While they were speeding off, one officer car came right behind them. The others followed as they embarked on a high-speed chase since they refused to stop. Meanwhile Darnel quickly called the ambulance as one of the officers stayed behind to help with Davina. He ran to his car to quickly grab a cloth and said "stay back!" to Darnel and Elizabeth who was hovering over Davina with terror in their eyes. He pushed them back as he tied a cloth around her arms and tied it tight. He then began CPR, with 30 compression then two breaths. He kept going until the ambulance came. They rushed out quickly and took over. One of the paramedics doing the CPR saw that she was still unresponsive and ordered one of his partners to get the AED, as he continued with the CPR.

The other paramedic moved Darnel and Elizabeth out of the scene. "I need to be there…" Elizabeth said.

"We can't do our job properly with you being there. We will do all we can to save her life; you both just have to stay out of the way." The Paramedic stopped the CPR when the AED was on the scene. He then quickly went with instruction, as he shocked her heart. After she didn't respond, he shocked her heart again then she gave a little response. They then put her on the bed inside the ambulance car and drove off, with Darnel and Elizabeth jumping inside the ambulance car. They hooked up the breathing machine on her as they drove her straight to the emergency room. They rushed her inside, as they made the parents wait in the lobby.

The chase was still going on while they were trying to save Davina's life. Allen ran into anything that was in his way but couldn't get them. They knew they had no choice but to call for more backups. The backup officers came towards them in an attempt to put the car chase to a stop before anybody got hurt. Minutes later during the chase, another officer's car was coming towards them. They escaped the first one, but they couldn't escape the second and third because they were both blocking the road with their cars.

"Man, what are we going to do?" Clayton asked Allen with panic in his voice.

"I'm running through this shit!" he said, as he ran one of the cars over as the other car hit him in the side, to put them at a complete stop. The car started smoking as they all surrounded them with guns in their hand.

"Come out with your hands up!" one of the officers commanded.

"Man, I can't go to jail..."

"I can't either, but we are trapped." He said looking around with blood coming from his head and down his face, as he was breathing heavily. "We are dead if we make any funny moves at this point."

"I will take my chances." Clayton said.

"No don't do it, surrender! we will find our way out."

"HOW MAN?"

"I don't know, just don't make no funny moves."

"Fuck that!" he opened the door to get out with a gun in his hand.

"NO!!" Allen said, while trying to pull him back.

"He got a gun!" one of the officers shouted, as he shot at the officers while trying to make a run for it. They fired back and did not stop until he was unresponsive on the ground. Allen stayed in the car and screamed "NO!!!" while putting both hands on the wheel where the officer could see. "Fuck!!!" he said as tears came down his eyes.

"Slowly come out of your vehicle with your hands up!" one of the officers commanded with frustration. They read him his rights and placed him under arrest after he got out of the car.

CHAPTER 38

"Hello, my name is Officer Carter, I am sure you remember me from last time." The officer said to Davina, who was handcuffed to her hospital bed.

"Yes."

"Before we start, do you need anything to drink?"

"No." She said with tears in her eyes, knowing it was over. There was no going back now, so she told him everything that happened.

"Davina, you are under arrest for the involvement of the death of Mrs. Lisa wood, Nita Price, and the wrongful imprisonment of Sia Singleton." He said as she sobbed even harder.

"Anything you say will be used against you in the court of law. You are entitled to a free lawyer if needed." He removed the handcuffs from the hospital bed and handcuffed her hands together behind her back, while her parents watched in agony.

"I will get you out of there as soon as I can, just hang in there." Darnel said.

"ok daddy." She cried as they took her away.

During an interview with Allen, he was being difficult with them knowing he would lose either way.

"So, tell us what happened the night of the fatal crash?" Officer Carter asked.

"There is nothing left for me to say, I thought the bitch already opened her wack ass mouth and told y'all everything."

"We just want to hear your part." Officer Leah who was also inside the interrogation room chimed in.

"And what's that going to do? Give me a free pass out of here? I doubt it."

"But it may give you a lesser charge." She said, still trying to convince him to talk.

Man, y'all stop playing with me like I'm stupid or something, get the fuck out of here with that shit."

"We just want to hear your part of the story, that's all. "Officer Carter said.

"I ain't got shit to tell y'all, so get me out of here."

"Ok then." Officer Carter said as they escorted him back to his cell.

"So now what?" Officer Leah said as she sighed.

"I don't know, but I think the only option we have is to get Davina and Allen in the same room; hopefully she will get him to talk."

"What are we waiting for then, let's go have a word with her."

"Sounds like a plan." Both officers jumped in the car and drove to where Davina was being held at.

They brought Davina into the interrogation room, but she didn't know what for this time.

"We brought you here to see what we can do to help each other." Officer Leah said.

"How?" Davina said with confusion.

"We have your boyfriend Allen in custody."

"He is not my boyfriend!" Davina said with a frown.

"Well, your ex-boyfriend." She was quiet and disgusted by just hearing his name.

"The reason you are here is to see if Allen will confess to you. If so, we will give you a lesser charge."

"How am I supposed to get him to confess to me? He just almost killed me!" she said furiously not understanding why they would want to put her life in danger again.

"You never know what he may say when he is in front of you. This is just an attempt to see if we can get something out of him."

"But what if I can't get him to confess?" she said, knowing Allen doesn't trust anybody. He would know this is a set up.

"Then your charges will still stand." Leah the detective said with a slight bit of irritation.

"I'm not doing it."

"Listen to me," officer Carter jumped in. "He may say something that will get you off big time. You are looking at seventeen years, but we can bring it down to five. So you don't think that's worth fighting for?"

"What if he tries to hurt me again?" she said, afraid of what he may do when he sees her again.

"With handcuffs on his hand really?" Leah said with more irritation in her tone.

"Ok, I don't feel comfortable talking to you anymore." Davina said to Officer Leah, then turned to Officer Carter "she needs to leave if you want me to even consider this."

"Ok that's fine, if that's what you want." He said, and then turned to Officer Leah "please excuse us."

"I will," she said then turned to Davina who was clearly frightened. "Just know one thing, we want him not you. So you being weak is not going to get us what we want to get you off." She said as she walked off.

"She is not trying to be mean; she just wants you to be strong enough to save yourself."

"How, when I'm still going to spend five years here even if he happens to confess to me which I doubt."

"Or seventeen years that was promised."

"I don't know."

"Ok then, it's up to you. Think about it and let us know what you want to do. If you don't do this, he will only be charged with attempted murder which will be a slap on the wrist. He will be a free man before you even dream about getting out. For all that is worth, think about your future." He said then had one of the officers take her back to her cell.

She thought about it for days and could not come to a conclusion on what to do, due to the fact she was still afraid of him. She never wanted to face him after what he did to her and her mother.

CHAPTER 39

Days later, her mother came to visit her.

"Where is dad?" Davina asked when she realized it was just her mother that came.

"He is at home. He is still trying to process the fact that you are in here."

"I know, I am too."

"How are you holding up here?"

"I am trying not to think about it, hopefully time will go by fast."

"I think accepting the fact that you are in here will make the time go even faster."

"I am not there yet, but I will get there eventually."

"I know you will darling."

"How is dad taking it?"

"Not well, but it's unfortunate that you being in here brought us closer together. He has been living in the house ever since and we have been closer than ever."

"I'm happy to hear that, but I have something to tell you." She said, feeling distant and uninterested of her dad moving back in when something bigger was weighing heavy in her heart.

"What is it sweetie?"

"They want me to talk to Allen."

"For what?" Elizabeth said with a frown on her face, but deep down her heart sunk when she heard those words.

"They want to see if I can get him to confess to lessen my charges to five years."

"That is very risky, but it sounds good."

"I know!"

"How can you get somebody that heartless, to tell you anything that could get them in deeper trouble to save you."

"That's what I am saying; he almost just killed me and you."

"I know, but he can't hurt you anymore; I'm sure they will have him handcuffed and make sure he doesn't come close to you to hurt you ever again."

"I don't know mom; I am really scared."

 "I know you are sweetie, but you will have to face him either way. Think about you for a change and do what it takes to save yourself this time.

"I don't know mom."

"You don't belong here; the loyalty you have for a man that didn't give two shits about you, got you here." She knew her mother was angry when she started to cuss.

"I will think about it."

"Ok then but think about your future sweetie."

"You sound like Officer Carter."

"He is right."

"I will let you know what I decide."

"Ok, but please do the right thing."

"Ok mother. And I am really happy you and dad are getting closer; it makes me happy to know my parents could possibly get back together." She said with a half-smile.

"Don't get too excited, we don't know yet. One step at a time."

"I'm ok with that."

"Just focus on what to do about Allen. But as your mother, I think you should do it. I will be in there if you need me to. I just hope I don't run up on him and smash his face on that table."

"That's the more reason you shouldn't be in there." They both cracked a mild laugh as she continued "I will do this on my own if I decide to go through with it." Davina concluded.

"Ok baby, let me know what you decide."

"I will mom, tell my dad to come see me and let him know I am ok."

"I will bring him with me next time."

"ok mom, thank you for coming."

"You're welcome darling." They hugged each other tight and long until the officer interrupted. "No touching."

"I will see you soon sweetie, stay strong and I love you."

"I love you too."

CHAPTER 40

A day later, she was escorted back to the interrogation room. She thought really hard and figured she had nothing to lose by facing him again. Allen was already in the room, not knowing why he was there this time. Davina saw him as she walked in, then froze. The feeling she had for him all came back, making her almost forget what he did to her. She quickly snapped out of it and turned those feelings to anger, remembering what he did to her, her mother, Sia and Nita.

"I see they got you too for opening your big ass mouth." Allen said to Davina, as they walked her in with handcuffs. She didn't say anything as they escorted her to a seat right across from where he was sitting at.

"So, are you just going to sit there like a deaf dummy?" he said when Davina did not respond after sitting down.

"You need to watch your fucking mouth on how you speak to me." She finally broke her silence.
"Oh I see you're still demanding respect like you deserve that shit." Allen said, then continued. "You ain't nobody but a snitching ass bitch. I could've ended your life the second I had the chance."
"You did have the chance remember, but your bitch ass failed you coward." She said out of the anger she was feeling, while looking at her ex-lover who recently ruined her life. He moved forward like he was going to hit her and she stood still. She was no longer afraid, knowing he couldn't hurt her anymore.
"Oh, you thought I'm still afraid of you after everything you put me through?"

"Wait till I get out of here, I am going to make you choke on every word. You should know better!" he said, but deep down he knew he had lost the hold he had on her.

"When will that be huh? because the only time you will be getting out of here is with a body bag. Let's just hope it's not soon." She threatened, trying to get a rise out of him.

"Is that a threat?" he said as he chuckled.

"There is no need to threaten you after all the mess you are in; you killed a pregnant woman and pinned it on an innocent girl you sick bastard!! And to even top it off, you killed another innocent girl all because she was getting to the truth." She said as her anger boiled up.

"I could've pinned it on your ass, maybe she would've been more loyal than your sorry ass. And Nita was the bitch you were supposed to keep in check, but you was too weak and stupid to do just that." He said with disgust in his eyes.

"For one, I was never sorry for telling the truth to free my friend. I can't believe I let you talk me into setting her up. And now you got rid of Nita too? You are a true monster." She looked him in the eye with some much hurt, as she refused to let the tear drop. "And by the way, thank you for your confession."

"I ain't gave you a goddamn thing." He said with anger, realizing he just confessed to the crimes.

"What do you call that huh?"

"Something to say to shut you the fuck up." He said as the anger brewed through his body, knowing he had fallen into their trap.

"You've done that for a long time, not anymore."

"You see I was trying to truly prevent myself from dating someone like my mother, but it seems like I just can't shake her out of my life." He said with disappointment as the officers walked in.

"I don't care about you or your fucking mother, I am just glad you are out of my life for good. And I'm sure she is somewhere regretting being your mother as we speak!" she said while they were taking her away. This time he was quiet, not knowing what to say or how to feel. He just knew it was over for him for good this time.

CHAPTER 41

It was a bright Tuesday morning on the day Sia was released; she took off her orange outfit and wore what her mother brought for her to wear home. She stepped outside as the sun gazed into her eyes. She covered her face with her right hand as she took a step towards the gate, hoping this was not one of her dreams. She took another step and another one until she got to the gate that opened up. Her mother and father were on the other side of the gate waiting for her. She jumped into her mother's arms and couldn't help but to cry.

Days went by before Sia left the house. The very first place she went to was Nita's grave to pay her respect with a flower. She sat there for a moment next to her grave before she could speak, trying to process her death. "There is nothing I can say right now to bring you back, it just hurts to know that you died because of my freedom." She said with tears coming down her chin. "I thank you for not giving up on me." She placed the flower on top of her grave then left.

Few more days had passed before Sia reached out to the family of Lisa, whose number she collected from one of the detectives in charge. She felt bad for their loss and wanted to let them know how sorry she was, although she was innocent. She offered her help to her husband whenever he needed help with the kids, knowing how hard it must be now raising the children on his own.

Sia walked in on a Thursday afternoon to the same prison cell she was locked up at, to face Davina.

"Do you remember the day we were playing in your backyard

when Danny and his mom came over?" Sia said to Davina "well that day, you told him you liked him and he told you he liked me and pushed you out of his way to talk to me. Do you remember what happened afterward?"

Davina tried to crack a smile knowing where she was getting at, "you took the bucket of sand and poured it on him and told him to leave us alone."

"And then what?"

"Then we ran inside."

"My point is, I have always had your back and you tried to ruin my life for the man you thought loved you? I loved you, I took you as my sister and had your back every step of the way. And you chose him over me?" she said with anger as Davina's head was down knowing what she had done. "I forgive you for my sake, I forgive you for the freedom you once took from me. I forgive you for almost ruining my life, but I will never forget what a friend you were to me."

"I'm so sorry!" she said in tears.

"Of course you are, you wouldn't be saying this if Nita didn't die for this." she said, then continued while Davina kept the tears coming "you could've prevented all of this if you just told the truth from the beginning."

"I was afraid!"

"Afraid of what? Of him going to jail?"

"No, he told me not to say anything and I thought he would do something to me if I did."

"I don't believe you were that afraid of him, you just lied to save his ass so you wouldn't be alone."

"No!" Davina responded, still in tears.

"It doesn't matter what you say, all I know is you gave up my life, Nita's life and now your life for him. I hope you can live with that." She said as she slammed the phone down and left without looking back.

The next day, she finally found the will to open the letter Tony sent her while she was in prison. She was afraid to see what he had to say about the situation. To her surprise, the letter made her smile and knew she still had a fighting chance with him.

www.ingramcontent.com/pod-product-compliance
Lightning Source LLC
Chambersburg PA
CBHW052015150726
47999CB00004B/1674